E!"

Black, furcovered batwings furled around her, attached to bony struts that were elongated metacarpels and phalanges. She had ten fingers on each hand; five supported the wing, the others were free, much like a human hand, even to the red lacquer on the fingernails.

Dalusa's face had a refined, sculpted beauty that could only have come from surgical alteration. An artist had wielded the scalpels.

. . . I felt a moment's bewilderment, unable to tell if she were a bat altered to look like a woman, or a woman attempting bathood.

"No! Don't touch me!" She leaped back, unfurling her wings with a rustle. "Do you see, you shook my hand. Your hand was damp, a little, and there are enzymes, oils, micro-organisms. . . ."

"I hurt you."

"It's nothing. It will go away in an hour. But can you see now why . . . I can never touch anyone. Or allow anyone to touch me."

. . . I felt a little weak. I had felt no real attraction to Dalusa when I first saw her, but at the news of her inaccessibility I felt a sudden lurch of desire. . . .

ABOUT THE COVER ARTIST(S)

Maintaining the "Discovery Series" policy of presenting new artists to complement the writings of new authors, the art that adorns the cover of this fourth volume is a striking example of the extraordinary talents of VISIONS GRAPHICS & FILM/L.A. The photograph and lettering were designed and art directed by Visions Graphics' collaborative partners, JOHN DAVID MOORE and MICHAEL D. GIBSON. The photograph was taken by Charles Bush.

This is the first book jacket for Visions, which is a relatively new design studio in Los Angeles. Moore and Gibson, ex-Art Center College of Design students, met in 1972 while assembling Moore's unusual one-man show of Sculptured Graphics in plastics and vinyls.

David—who was originally from Canada—came to California in 1968 to study architecture and later environmental design and graphics. But during the course of his formal education his talent was inexorably drawn to the creation of non-categorizable art on a totally spontaneous level. The nature of these art "happenings" (specifics are now buried in the dust of days past) served to alienate the college administrators, though the students related to David's work; so he quickly moved out of architecture, furniture, and interiors, and into graphics and fine art.

At the time of their meeting, Michael had been painting auto-
motive designs on formula racing cars. He was a former
track runner and successful Motocross racer, but like David,
had been drifting toward visuals. This new type of modern
graphics seemed an entrance to the world of serious art.

Michael attended the Art Center also, as a student of graphics
and film. But the outside business he and David had started
became too time-consuming to permit the continuation of formal
schooling. And so, for the last four years plus—they have
been the core of Visions Graphics & Film. To say their success
has been phenomenal is to understate criminally.

Their special look on record album covers is legendary, and
their graphics have been acknowledged as instrumental in
pushing albums by such talents as Ray Charles, Stevie Wonder
and Rare Earth into the million sellers. But albums are only
part of the Visions Graphics repertoire. Motion picture post-
ers: a recent example is the Voyage Productions poster for the
Fantastic Animation Festival. Animated film titles: the concept
for the new CBS logo; film title sequence for the latest Elektra/
Asylum Records movie; logo for the new TV series International
Disco; endless still logos and TV commercials.

Now hip-deep in the application of a singular animation technique of their own devising, they are hard at work applying
it to a feature-length fantasy film they have written.

They both live and work in a large rambling house that con-
tains their studios and workshops in Eagle Rock, a suburb of Los
Angeles. They, like the editor of this series, are proud of
this first venture into book covers. If you stopped to check
out INVOLUTION OCEAN, never having heard of Bruce Sterling,
it was certainly because of the dynamic design vision of Visions
Graphics.

INVOLUTION
OCEAN

Bruce Sterling

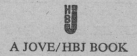

A JOVE/HBJ BOOK

First Jove/HBJ edition published January 1977

Library of Congress Catalog Card Number: 77-80694

Cover art and lettering designed by Visions Graphics & Film,
Los Angeles/John David Moore and Michael D. Gibson.
Cover photograph by Charles Bush.

Printed in the United States of America.

───

Jove/HBJ books are published by Jove Publications, Inc.
(Harcourt Brace Jovanovich) 757 Third Avenue, New York,
N.Y. 10017

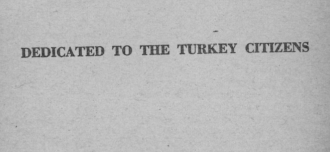

DEDICATED TO THE TURKEY CITIZENS

A FINENESS OF 0.995

an introduction by
HARLAN ELLISON

The memorable created worlds: Frank Herbert's Dune
world, Ray Bradbury's Mars, Jack Vance's Big Planet,
Arthur C. Clarke's Rama, Edgar Rice Burrough's Barsoom,
Michael Moorcock's Melniboné. Add to them now, in an
absolutely stunning *tour de force* by a writer barely into his
twenties, Nullaqua. The bizarre and eerily fatal dustworld,
Nullaqua.

What lies ahead for you, gentle reader, in the following
pages, is a genuinely revelatory experience. Nullaqua and
its inhabitants—human and otherwise—will not soon be
flensed from your memory. I use the whaling term "flense"
to maintain the idiom of the novel. It is the perfect word, in
this case. Look it up; it's a super word. As *Involution
Ocean* is a super novel. As its author, Bruce Sterling, is a
super writer in the sense of extraordinary, above, beyond,
superior, supernal.

Superb.

The former standard of fineness for gold in the United
Kingdom was 0.995, and it was interpreted in terms of the
pound sterling. Sterling means of excellent fineness. Heavy-
handed, I lumber toward the point: Bruce Sterling is a
writer of excellent fineness. In point of fact, I am somewhat
awed by his abilities.

The admission does not come easily to me. A recogni-
tion of the reality that already, at this preliminary stage of
what I perceive as one of the most promising writing ca-
reers in years, this kid does things I cannot do after twenty-
two years laboring at my craft. In his first novel he has

reached a level of skill and invention that it took me over ten years to *begin* to work at.

None of this is proffered as hype. Those of you who have purchased the first three books in this series have come to trust my judgment on these "Discovery" volumes, and were I to try passing off a clinker as 0.995, I would hear about it *ad perpetuam rei memoriam*. In the case of this book, I am utterly secure in my feeling that you will be amazed and delighted.

But though the book speaks for itself, a thumpingly good read with characters that dance in the memory and events that are singular for their originality and execution, it is the author and how he came to you, and to me, that adds a fillip of wonder to the mere holding of *Involution Ocean* in your hands.

Let me tell you about Sterling. Fine, fine, superfine Sterling.

I met him on April 14th, 1974. It was his twentieth birthday.

Deeply enmeshed in the web of a new romance, I had taken a wild flight from Los Angeles to College Station, Texas, in the company of that April Temptress, strictly as a lark. It was spring, I was stunned by present passion. A bunch of my Texas friends were holding a regional convention—the Aggie-Con—and I said what the hell. So we flew to dreary College Station, surely the least romantic spot on the face of the Earth. I say this because I have never been to Ulanbaatar, the capitol of Mongolia. But until I *have,* College Station beats out Springfield, Ohio, for the title.

Now, for those of you who don't understand Bruce Sterling's dedication to this book, permit me to explain the "Turkey City Writers' Workshop." It figures prominently, honest to God.

As I noted in an introduction to an anthology of science fiction by Texas writers, *Lone Star Universe* (Heidelberg Publishers, 1976, 313 pages, $9.95, and a swell book it is, for the most part, with a keen Sterling short story in-

10

cluded), the last ten years have seen the emergence of a surprising number of first-rank sf talents from the Texas axis. Steven Utley, Howard Waldrop, Joe Pumilia, Lisa Tuttle, Jake Saunders; Tom Reamy and H.H. Hollis, both of whom tragically, died this year; and others. And because this group of people *like* each other, unlike most "salons" of writers, they get together for half-baked Clarion/Milford-style sessions of mutual criticism during which stories or newly completed work is work-shopped and the writers' strengths or flaws are brought under microscopic scrutiny. These sessions occur whenever three or more Texas writers find themselves at the same point in space, the same instant in time. With charming lack of self-importance, they call these sessions "Turkey City Workshops." Hey, one will say to another, let's have a Turkey City. And so they do.

Well, a Turkey City had been called for the 1974 Aggie-Con. The guest of honor, a well-known sf author, had been asked to sit in on the session and, since I was coming, they asked me if I'd join in.

Well again, I arrived with the April Temptress on a rickety feeder flight out of Dallas-Ft. Worth, in a single-engine propper that might well have served as the flagship of the South Mollucan National Airlines (slogan: "Your Cattle-Car in the Sky") and was quickly hustled into a Turkey City set-up with Tuttle, Utley, Pumilia, Waldrop and other Hugo and Nebula award winners, not to mention the famous Guest of Honor, who turned out to be a swine, insulted everyone, and hobbled out of the workshop to the relief of everyone present.

I had been given a stack of manuscripts when I arrived. They were the stories that were to be discussed. I had to read them quickly, but as the comments were being voiced around the workshop circle I was able to steal time to re-read the stories I'd skimmed.

There were the usual sword & sorcery droppings, one or two artsy pastiches, several "hard science" boredoms, and a couple of fantasies. The traditional offscourings of such literary get-togethers. But the level of criticism was high, as was to be expected from writers of such quality. There

11

were a few people in the circle whom I didn't know, however.

One of them was a young man, extremely slim, about five ten, brown eyes and hair, weighing about 140, good-looking in a farmboy sort of way, thin and tight around the eyes and mouth, as though extremely wary of the company he was keeping. He was introduced as Bruce Sterling, a writer who had never sold any of his work, a writer who had only recently begun to hang out with the Texas writers, a writer who had been writing only a short time, though he had been into sf and fantasy since his discovery of Edgar Rice Burroughs at the age of eleven. His comments about other people's stories were short and sharp and to the point. But I didn't pay much attention to him. There were some budding superstars in the group, and most of them were my friends; one of them was a long-time protegee.

When it came time to workshop Sterling's story, a ten-page, 2,250-word short titled "Living Inside," I discovered that it had been overlooked in my skimming. So as the comments started around the circle, I began reading rapidly.

In the circle were four or five writers who had submitted stories to *The Last Dangerous Visions*—it'll be published by Harper & Row in late 1978, friends—and two of them had sold to the book. But even though the others hadn't hit the book, they were excellent young writers, and their mouths watered to be a part of that showcase anthology. And as I read Sterling's story, I heard them criticizing it:

"This is a piece of shit, Bruce," said one. Then he went on to detail its alleged shittiness.

"Gawdawful, Bruce," said another, who had tried to hit TLDV on three separate occasions and had failed each time. "At least you've managed to get a little characterization in this one, but it's no better than all the others we've seen."

"It's stupid and pointless," said a third.

One or two people had moderately affirmative things to say about "Living Inside," but for the most part the story took a terrible drubbing at the hands and mouths of the Texas axis. (Understand: this was not random viciousness, but informed and precisely to the point analysis. They really did not like the story, and they had understandable plot and structure reasons for their dislike. Standard workshop technique, acceptable in every way.)

Now the comments had worked around to me. They had saved me for last, because I was the longest-established professional there, and I had taught Clarion Workshops some of them had attended.

I looked around the circle. The dramatic pause. They watched me, hoping I would do one of my famous, patented tearing-up-the-manuscript-and-flinging-it-in-the-face-of-the-offending-author routines. Cheap thrills. Lisa Tuttle half-smiled. Steve Utley looked comatose, but that's usual. Pumilia and Saunders and Waldrop waited expectantly: I'd savaged their work several times. Sterling stared across at me as placid and unconcerned as a cow going to the maul. They all knew I'd hate the story and would rip up this presumptuous kid who had had the *chutzpah* to enter his miserable sophomoric work in the company of his betters.

"If you'll permit me the honor," I said to Sterling, "I'd like to buy this story for *The Last Dangerous Visions*. I think it's damned near brilliant."

The wonders of peripheral vision. I *saw*, all in a moment: Lisa Tuttle's mouth drop open; Joe Pumilia slip half off his chair; Utley's eyes blink a thousand times in an instant; Howard Waldrop put his hand to his suddenly gaping maw; everyone else starting with involuntary twitches and tremors. The wonders of full-perimeter hearing. I *heard*, all in that moment: "Jeezus Kee-wry-st!" from one of them; "Gah-*damn*" from another; "Whaaaat?" from a third; "Holy shit," from another. And gasps, and squeals, and disbelief, and stammering, and envy, and choking. And then, in the next instant: absolute joy and delight!

They are good *good* kids, those Texas writers.

And they started congratulating Bruce Sterling, all of them at once, smiling and laughing and just pleased as hell that he had made his first sale, right before their eyes.

Then they demanded I explain *why* I thought it was such a smashingly good piece of work. Which I did. And you can find out for yourself when you buy *The Last Dangerous Visions* next year.

But here's the *amazing* thing.

Bruce Sterling never batted an eye. When I asked him if he'd take 2¢ a word, $68, for the use of the story, he nodded and said softly, "That'll be okay, I guess."

Cool? Was he cool? Was that goddam kid cool? Let me *tell* you how cool he was. Unruffled, unperturbed, unshaken, just twenty years old that day, he was the most professional person in the room, including me.

Bruce tells me now that he was a naive, frightened, romantic adolescent, totally out of his depth with writers who had been working in the field for years and who had garnered the highest awards. But he didn't *seem* to be any of that. He was laid back, professional, apparently unconcerned at this startling sudden change in the direction of his life. At that moment when an editor said, yes, you have talent, and I'll pay you for the privilege of backing up my opinion in print . . . he passed over a line. From unknown to professional. He had long before that time passed over the line from amateur to unknown, which are very different things indeed. But right then, right there, at that moment, the world was open to Bruce Sterling. He could now be anything he wanted to be, because he had a singular, individual, recognizable, marketable, freedom-affording talent. It was one of those pivot points in our lives that we often don't recognize till we're years past them.

But here it was, and *everyone* recognized it, and Bruce Sterling took it as calmly as if he'd asked them to pass the butter. At least, that's the way it *looked*.

Bruce tells me now that he was stunned. He knew nothing about the way in which writers submit stories for publication. He had, in fact, written the story as something of a lark. He had been writing incredibly complex sf plots till that time, and he thought "Living Inside" was too simple to be much good. He had written it so he could have something new to submit to the Turkey City at the AggieCon.

He never thought it would sell. Never thought, in fact, that it would rate anything higher than the abuse it had received from everyone else in that circle.

Bruce tells me now that he was knocked out.

But miGod he was cool at that moment.

Hemingway once said that guts is "grace under pressure."

Bruce Sterling is one of the gutsiest people I've ever met.

Michael Bruce Sterling was born in Brownsville, Texas April 14, 1954. His parents were Marion Bruce Sterling (also called "Bruce") and Gloria Vela Sterling. They were both natives of South Texas. Their collective ancestry included Spanish, Italian, Dutch, English, Scottish, and Amerindian elements.

Sterling's parents moved to Austin when he was six months old. The elder Sterling got his degree in mechanical engineering at the University of Texas at Austin. Then the family moved to the Galveston area. Bruce spent his formative years there, where the Texas petrochemical industry put bread into his mouth by profiting at the expense of the environment.

He says of himself that he was "a reclusive little geek who routinely made 'U's in conduct and penmanship."

Over the years Sterling's family was enlarged by the birth of two sisters (now dead) and a brother. When Sterling was nine, his family bought a ranch in Schulenburg, Texas. Weekends there were a great release from the technological Atlantis of the Texas City-LaMarque area. (Atlantis in fact, for the entire area is now sinking beneath the weight of industrial subsidization.)

He started writing at the age of twelve in what he calls "a frank bid for attention."

During his first semester of high school his family decided to move to India to take part in a fertilizer plant project. He was fifteen at the time. He spent two and a half years overseas, travelling extensively. Although, he says, he was too withdrawn to try to understand the alien culture, he did fall victim to the appeal of the Romantic poets.

At seventeen, while waiting in the dusty Madras airport for a plane from the airline that was eventually to wipe out half his family, Bruce Sterling got the inspiration for *Involution Ocean*, what would later become his first novel.

After completing high school by correspondence, Sterling was unanimously voted Most Popular by his senior class. The vote was 1-0.

He went to college at his father's alma mater, UT Austin. In Austin, the hopelessly alienated Sterling, suffering from culture shock of the rawest sort, discovered a group of what he calls "sickies who made even my afflictions seem minor . . . they were science fiction fans."

With the encouragement of the Turkey City circle, he began writing seriously. In 1974, at age twenty, success fell on him; dropped like a giant golden meadow muffin by the Cordwainer Bird, as reported earlier in these comments.

Since that time, three years have ticked away at college. Perhaps the climax of his scholastic career was his involvement in the Absurdist Takeover of the University of Texas Student Government. In 1976 he graduated with a bachelor's degree in journalism. He also acquired several unnamed vices and a most splendiferous woman companion named Nancy, with whom he currently lives in Austin.

Other minor data: he was a Clarion Workshop student in the Summer of 1974, attending on a scholarship funded by a well-known writer whose annual selection of a single student is based on talent alone. He types on a Royal portable. He admires the work of Philp José Farmer, Thomas Pynchon, R.A. Lafferty, Roger Zelazny, Jorge Luis Borges, Larry Niven, and a host of others. He reads rather too heavily in the genre for this editor's taste, but he thinks it's "a gas" (touching phrase), and has a naive idealism about science fiction that many of us find, well, touching. Also pathetic.

As for *Involution Ocean*, Sterling claims that his major influences were Clark Ashton Smith, Larry Niven, Samuel Taylor Coleridge, and yours truly, whom he insists I say supplied at least half of the plot. This last statement, though set down as ordered, is pure, unadulterated Texican bullshit.

The kid did it on his own.

He is now twenty-three years old.

Eat your hearts out, you old farts who've been writing for thirty-five years and can't cut what he has done here.

I first saw *Involution Ocean* as a short story. It was one of the pieces Bruce submitted during my week teaching at the 1974 Clarion Writers' Workshop in Fantasy and Science Fiction at Michigan State University. It was a repeat of the AggieCon Turkey City scene.

Bruce worked like crazy to write a story longer than the usual two to three thousand worders the students have time to write each week of the six-week workshop. It was thirty-five or forty pages in length and he had titled it—with an almost palpable desire to be crucified by his compatriots—"Moby Dust."

He was not disappointed. The other students ravaged the story, calling it a stupid imitation of Melville. When the time came for my comments, as the Enthroned Gray Eminence, I said simply, "Bruce, if you'll rewrite and expand this story to 60,000 words, and change that moronic title, I'd be very honored to publish this as one of the 'Harlan Ellison Discovery Series'."

The sound of bodies hitting the floor was only slightly louder than the sounds of jaws dropping. Sterling had done it again. And again, he was cool. "Sure, that'll be okay," he said.

And now, three years later, here it is.

He wrote it two years ago, when he was twenty-one, but publishing schedules and the crazed pattern of the editor's life has kept it from you an additional twenty-four months.

But consider: here is a first novel written by a twenty-one-year-old, that has all the maturity and depth and power of work turned out by men and women twenty and more years his senior.

17

If you get the message that I am in awe of Bruce Sterling's talent and craft and promise, you get the message clearly.

It is a joy to me that I have been in any way responsible for setting this remarkable piece of fiction in your path.

I could write on for another five thousand words about the background of Nullaqua that Bruce has created, a world both familiar and alien, and fully formed so you can see it, feel it, live in it. There is a paen I could raise to the individuality of the characters—John Newhouse in all his odd complexity, with motivations at once both obvious and murky; the unforgettable Dalusa, surely one of the most memorable aliens ever created in this genre (and I hope to God someone asks Larry Niven to review this book, because he'll *love* her); Captain Desperandum (oh, Christ, how I love that name!) and his strange secret desire for forbidden knowledge; the residents of the New House in the Highisle; Dumonty Calothrick and the fanatical Murphig—not to mention the alien creatures who inhabit that bizarre ocean of dust without bottom, set within a crater whose walls are seventy miles high.

Oh my, how I envy your reading this novel for the first time!

And the writing itself! How lean, how pure and direct. Sheer excellence at storytelling. It sings, it soars, it lifts on easy wings. This is a man who knows how to put one word in front of another, to carry you along effortlessly.

Nor do not be gulled into thinking this is a *roman à clef* imitating *Moby Dick*. Apart from the grace of the prose and a certain unnameable tone that harkens back to Melville's way of suffusing that grand novel with a metaphysical ambience, there is no relation. This is no obsessed Ahab stalking a demon beast. No *Orca*, no *Jaws*, no *Old Man and the Sea*. This is *Involution Ocean*, all its own thing, all its own property. Flense your mind of all preconceptions, I beg you.

And let me detain you no longer.

Go. Rush inside and marvel at this kid named Sterling, 0.995 fine, who writes like a cynical angel. It isn't often, gentle reader, that we have the opportunity to get in at the beginning of a career this promising. We owe it not so much to Sterling, but to ourselves, to make sure nothing gets in this man's way as he tells his stories. He enriches us.

HARLAN ELLISON
East Lansing, Michigan
9 July 77

CONTENTS

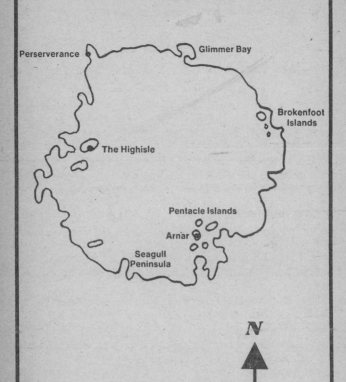

Perserverance

Glimmer Bay

Brokenfoot
Islands

The Highisle

Pentacle Islands

Arn'ar

Seagull
Peninsula

N

Nullaqua

Chapter 1

An Unfortunate Occurrence and Its Remedy

We all have some emptiness in our lives, an emptiness that some fill with art, some with God, some with learning. I have always filled the emptiness with drugs.

Because of this I found myself, duffel bag in hand, ready to go on a whaling voyage on that obscure planet, Nullaqua.

The Nullaquan dustwhale is the only source of the drug syncophine. At the time of my voyage, knowledge of this fact was becoming more and more widely spread. Because I had learned it, I, John Newhouse, was living with nine others on 488 Piety Street in the Highisle, Nullaqua's largest city.

The two-story metal building was known simply as the New House to us, its inhabitants. We were a motley group; the only things uniting us were our extra-Nullaquan origins and our connoisseur's delight in Flare, the initiate's term for syncophine. We were all human beings or close facsimiles thereof. First among us was white-haired old Timon Hadji-Ali. Timon never told us his age, but he was obviously at that period when the body's own subconscious wish to die begins to take precedence over the ego's desire for life. I often heard him speak of his friendship, centuries ago, with Ericald Svobold, the legendary discoverer of syncophine. Now, however, pessimism had overcome old Timon, and for years he had refused any rejuvenation. He wanted only to spend the last of his life depleting his slowly amassed capital and savoring Flare's fierce brain-kick. In matters of policy concerning our little group, we usually deferred to him as he still had the most money.

Second was Agathina Brant, a large, muscular woman with a ramrod posture. She was evidently a retired military officer, and she was extremely terse, even sullen. She almost always wore a uniform, clean but old. There was no telling which one of humanity's numberless armies had issued it. She never told us; I suspect that she sewed it herself. Her addiction was extremely strong.

Third and fourth were a married couple, Mr. and Mrs. Undine. Her maiden name was Stuart; his, Foster. They also were quite old. One could tell their age from their unnatural grace and the occasional archaisms in their speech. They were handsome people, if you discounted their barrel chests and the rather tasteless jewelry grafted into their bodies. As they never tired of telling us, they had both lived through several marriages and could not stand the idea of the pain involved in breaking up their latest one. They had resolved to commit suicide together, preferably by overdose. Many times I was tempted to advise them to use a poison other than syncophine, but that, I thought, might be a boorish invasion of their privacy.

The fifth of our company was a poet named Simon. Through cosmetic surgery he had acquired a kind of haggard handsomeness, although his eyes were of different colors. In an attempt to "return to the roots" as he told us, he had bought a primitive stringed instrument and was trying to teach himself to play it, in order to accompany himself while chanting his own works. We had soundproofed his upstairs room. Syncophine, he said, "stimulated his brain." There was certainly no denying that.

Simon was accompanied by a mousy woman named Amelia, who had long brown hair parted severely in the middle. Her father was a scholar, and sent her enough money for her own support and that of her quasi-melodious companion. She had lived with us for a month before trying syncophine. Now she was developing a taste for it.

Our seventh was a neuter, Daylight Mulligan. It was a charming conversationalist, and its speech revealed a great breadth of knowledge. It and I might have become close

24

friends were it not for its extreme paranoia regarding anyone possessing organs of reproduction. It itself had, of course, been neatly cloned, and its suspicions had some justification in that it had a definite sexual appeal for members of both sexes. It was often melancholy, perhaps tormented by guilt. The antique Timon told me once that it had been responsible for the double suicide of a married couple, friends of its, who both wanted to commit—or attempt to commit—adultery with it. This may or may not have been true.

Our eighth was an extremely tall, almost cadaverous woman named Quade Altman. Born on a planet with a gravity half that of Nullaqua, or of Earth for that matter, she approached eight feet. She was always pale, her sunken eyes ringed with delicate blues and purples. She often complained of dizzy spells. She spent a lot of time supine, working on her three-dimensional mosaics.

Ninth and next to last was my own mistress of the moment, Millicent Farquhar. Millicent was short, snub-nosed, red-haired, closer to plump than thin. I had met her on Reverie a year before, just before going to Nullaqua. After a particulary abandoned party, I had awakened to find myself in her bed. We had been introduced, but we had forgotten one another's names. Our mutual rediscovery had been very pleasant, and we had spent the last year in something like contentment.

Last, me, John Newhouse. Understand that I am not the same person who underwent the adventures I am about to describe. The personality is a changing, fleeting thing, and except for a few memories, now blurring, I have nothing to do with the man who called himself by my name at that time.

But that John Newhouse, then, was the son of a lumber baron on the planet Bunyan and was as well educated as that planet could manage. For political reasons and those of vanity, I claimed to have been born on Earth. Like most sectarian planets, Nullaqua has an exaggerated respect for anything Terran. The lie helped.

I was five feet ten inches tall and had very dark hair, growing rather sparse in the back, although I refused to

25

admit it. I parted it on the left. My eyes were also dark, and the left one had a slight grayish spot, almost a cataract, where I had once ill-advisedly dropped syncophine optically. I was pale from long amounts of time spent indoors, but I was capable of tanning very deeply. My nose had perhaps too pronounced a hook to be called handsome. I was—let me confess it—somewhat of a dandy, and I was fond of wearing rings, usually five at a time. I owned two dozen. I was thirty-five—forgive me, reader, have I not sworn honesty—I was forty-three standard years old.

I will not name my father. I took the name Newhouse from my abode, as was once the custom on Earth. Before my whaling voyage, I earned my living exporting high-quality syncophine to my numerous friends back on Reverie. While not spectacularly profitable, it was a pleasant way to spend one's time. My hobby was developing cheaper and more efficient ways of extracting syncophine from the basic oil.

It was a snug, almost smug existence. Then came disaster.

The expansion of the syncophine trade had not gone unnoticed. The bureaucrats of the Confederacy, that loose and steadily weakening association of worlds, issued a decree. Nullaqua heard, and, amazingly, obeyed.

We first heard of the news from our dealer, a Nullaquan named Andaru. Andaru was a retired whaler, and he supplied us with what he called gut oil at an almost nominal fee. There was no other demand for the product; the intestinal oil could not be burned, and Nullaquans refused to eat it, deeming it poisonous. More fools they, we thought.

On the seventeenth day of the tenth month of the year, Andaru knocked at the door and I answered it.

"It's Andaru," I said loudly to the rest, who were eating in the kitchen.

"Good. Wonderful. Fantastic," they all said. Their moods never failed to alter for the better at the prospect of another gallon.

"And there's someone with him," I continued more quietly, as a young man with a sharp nose and blond hair like tangled nylon stepped out from behind the Nullaquan and extended his hand. I shook it.

"Hi, I'm Dumonty Calothrick, just call me Monty," he said cheerfully. "Just dropped in from off planet, heard of the opportunities here, y'know—" Here he winked broadly at me and made a quick squeezing motion with the thumb and forefinger of his right hand where Andaru was unable to see. "I kind of asked around, met your friend here, thought I might come along, kind of seek you out, maybe," here a look of ingenous bewilderment "maybe ask your advice?"

"Come in, please, and seat yourselves," I said. "Wait . . . have you eaten?"

"Yes," said the Nullaquan. "No, sure haven't," Calothrick said.

"Right through there, then, please," I said, "Pick up a plate and introduce yourself to the rest of the household while I discuss business with our mutual acquaintance."

"Thank you, Mr. Uh . . ."

"Newhouse," I said, waving him on.

"Ain't you gonna eat, John?" Andaru said.

"I've eaten," I lied. It was Agathina Brant's turn to cook, and it damaged my digestion to witness the woman's heresies with food. I have always prided myself on my ability with what the Terrans used to call *le good cuisine*.

"How much did you bring?" I asked.

" 'Bout a gallon, as usual. 'Fraid it's the last one you're gonna get."

"Oh?" I said. "That's a shock, Andaru. Are you leaving the business?"

"I got to. It's illegal now."

Ice grew in my veins at the words. "Who says so?" I said.

"The Confederacy does; heard the news just yesterday."

"The Confederacy?" I repeated numbly.

"Yeah, the Confederacy, you know, skinny little fellows that float between the stars and tell folks how to get along."

"But they have no authority over plenetary affairs"

"Well, they made Nullaqua what you might call a polite request."

27

"And Nullaqua obeyed it."

"Why not? We got nothing to lose by being nice to the Confederacy as far as I can see."

I saw a slim ray of hope. "But you have something to lose, though."

"Yeah, there's that," he admitted, "but listen, they say some folks have been using this gut oil to make *drugs* with."

"No! You don't say!" I said. The bucolic Nullaquans have virtually no concept of drug abuse, sticking to tobacco and cheap beer.

"What wonderful food!" came the sudden voice of Dumonty Calothrick from the kitchen. I grimaced.

"So this is our last gallon."

"Yep. Everyone I know who sells it is closin' up shop."

"They don't want to break the law."

"They sure don't. That's a sin."

I knew better than to press the old Nullaquan. Besides, he had all the native's aversion to water, and, unlike him, I did not have a thick, puffy growth of hair in my nostrils to filter out unpleasantness. "How much for this last jug, then?"

"One monune and thirty-six pennigs."

"Right you are," I said, counting out the money onto his calloused palm. We exchanged expressions of mutual esteem. I opened the door for him and he left.

Then I sat down slowly on the comfortless whalehide couch to think things over. I felt a sudden itch for a quick blast of Flare, but, unlike the others, I kept my cravings rigidly under control.

"When you've finished eating come in here," I shouted. "I've got news."

I took the jug in my lap and pried the lid off. I sniffed. It was the usual high-quality stuff. I resealed it.

They were out in three minutes. "Bad news, "I said. "The Confederacy has declared Flare illegal and Nullaqua is going along. This—" I thumped it— "is our last jug."

Their faces fell in unison. It was a disturbing sight. We turned to Timon for advice. "I—" he began.

"Oh well, I've got a little bit here with me, let's do up

some," Calothrick interrupted brightly. He took a plastic packet out of the breast pocket of his checkered shirtjac and pulled an eyedropper out of his belt. The group quickly shuffled themselves into a circle on the carpet as Calothrick opened the packet and sucked up a dropperful of the liquid.

Timon frowned. "I suggest we ration what we have left. If the Nullaquans refuse to supply us we will have to send out one of our number to get it for us. Straight from the source. From a whale."

Daylight Mulligan clapped its hands. "Bravo, Timon," it said. Mrs. Undine passed it the dropper; it opened its mouth and squirted a quick blast onto its tongue.

"Which one of us?" said Quade Altman, in falsetto.

"Well, the women are out," said Mr. Undine. "I hear that whalers don't allow them on board."

"So will someone have to make the complete trip?" said Simon the poet, his brain now well stimulated.

"Oh, yes," said Timon. "And as they last six months, I suggest we choose someone as quickly as possible. Toward the end things may grow uncomfortable." Simon and Amelia both looked suddenly frightened. Mr. and Mrs. Undine held hands.

"I nominate John Newhouse," said Agathina Brant suddenly. Everyone looked startled; she spoke so seldom.

"Let's draw straws," I said quickly.

"John, you're the best choice," said Mr. Undine, in obvious relief. "You have the resilience of youth, certainly."

I countered, "But you have the experience of age. Surely that counts for more."

"But you have sharp wits. And resourcefulness. None of us can deny that," said Simon.

"Yes, Simon, but think how your poetry could gain from the trip," I said.

"But you have experience. You know what oil to get and how to brew it," Daylight Mulligan said. It had me there. More than anything else, this sealed my fate.

Things looked black. Surely, I thought, Millicent will defend me. I looked at her.

"Yes, and you can get a job, John," she said. "You can

29

cook. You're a good cook. You won't have any trouble."

"Let's not reach any hasty conclusions," I said. "Perhaps we should reconsider our situation in a week. It might be possible—"

Then Dumonty Calothrick spoke up. "Why wait? It's wonderful!" he laughed. "No sooner does the problem arise than it is solved. Think, Mr. Newhouse, the lure of adventure, the thrill of an alien planet. Six months before the mast. New sights! New thrills! Romance! Flare by the gallon! Hey, anybody want another quick blast?"

"Why don't *you* go?" I asked gently.

"Oh, I am, I am! I'm going with you!"

Chapter 2
Boarding Ship

The entire habitable portion of Nullaqua lies at the bottom of a monster crater some seventy miles deep and, for the most part, five hundred miles across. Over 90 percent of the planet's atmosphere lies pooled in this vast hollow; the rest of the planet has only a thin scattering of gases and the ruins of two Elder Culture outposts. According to accepted theory, the crater was gouged by a concentrated bombardment of antimatter meteors some billions of years ago. It would have splattered a younger planet but at that time Nullaqua was solid almost to the core. Vast volumes of gas were liberated from the broken rock. After that, the multiple tons of fine dust, caused by the action of the sun on Nullaqua's almost airless surface, sifted or were blown into the crater. This gradual but ceaseless action, continuing even today, has given Nullaqua an ocean of almost monatomic dust, untold miles deep. Nullaqua was given a second chance to create life. This time, she succeeded.

Five hundred years ago Nullaqua was settled by a dour group of religious fanatics. Their creed is now somewhat weakened, but still retains its colorful blasphemies and an exaggerated respect for the law.

It was that respect that now forced me to leave the comfort of my double bed to seek my fortune on the Sea of Dust. With me was young Calothrick; I was unable to dissuade him from coming.

I walked sullenly out of the New House, Calothrick tagging at my heels. We headed toward the docks east of the city. After two blocks he broke the silence.

31

"What's our first step, Mr. Newhouse?"

"To take all our money out of the bank," I said. "And call me John."

"OK, John. Why? Aren't we going to sign up?"

"This is not a course of action to be rushed into blindly," I said, speaking with excessive clarity. "We have to study the situation, learn the basics of the industry, and some of the slang of the sailors. We have to buy supplies, probably get our hair cut in the current sea-dog style. We have to look like we know what's what, even if we are off-worlders. As it is you may have trouble getting a berth. You'll have to sign on as an ordinary seaman."

"Ordinary seamen, huh? Well, that's all right with me. I wouldn't want to be better than anyone else."

"Sure," I said. "How much money do you have?"

Calothrick looked startled and unsure. "Not very much. About five hundred monunes."

"That should be enough for your supplies, anyway, with maybe enough left over to buy drinks for the sailors. What's your bank?"

"I haven't had time to deposit it yet, it's all in letters of credit."

I sent Calothrick off to pick up some cash while I rented a room in a tavern at the lip of the cliff above the docks. (The Highisle was half a mile above sea level and thus escaped the worst of the dust pollution below.)

When Calothrick returned I sent him downstairs to buy drinks for sailors and to study their mannerisms. I went out and bought two dustmasks. All sailors wear them. The fine dust, stirred by gusts of wind, can destroy the lungs within a few days. Even the dense thickets of hair in the native Nullaquan's nostrils can't fully filter the stuff, nor can their camellike lashes and thick lids fully shield their eyes. On shore they suffice, but at sea every man jack wears a tight-fitting rubbery mask with a snoutlike round filter and round plastic eyes.

The captain and his mates give their orders through speakers connected to tiny microphones within their masks. The crew have no speakers inside their masks, as any power of speech among them would be superfluous.

32

Every whaler has a painted insignia on the forehead and cheeks of his mask. They vary wildly in shape and color; it is one of their few modes of self-expression. I bought several tubes of paint and some brushes for Calothrick and myself. The mask's natural color is shiny black, so I bought some black paint, too. It might be just as well to be able to suddenly change insignias. After all, one learns to recognize a whaler by his dustmask.

After buying sailor's garb and cutting our hair, Calothrick and I took the elevator down the cliffside to look over the whaling fleet. We took our dufflebags and our alien's papers. The first three ships would have nothing to do with us. They were willing to accept me as cook, but not with Calothrick, who was an obvious ignoramus.

Finally we came across the good ship *Lunglance*, commanded by one Nils Desperandum. Desperandum, an obvious alias, was also an off-worlder. He was an immense man, raised under at least two gravities.

Though he was only five feet tall, with his incredible bulk and thick blond beard Desperandum had a commanding presence. He looked us over. "Cook and ordinary seaman?" he asked sharply.

"Uh . . . aye aye, sir," Calothrick began, but I cut him off with a quick "Yes, sir."

"Any objection to sailing with other off-worlders? We don't go strictly by the book on this vessel."

"None at all, Captain, if they don't mind sailing with us."

"Very well, sign yourselves on. Cook's lay is one one-twenty-fifth. Mr. Calothrick, I'm afraid that the best I can offer you is the three-hundredth lay. But there'll be a bonus if the cruise goes well."

Calothrick's face clouded but I cut in before he could offer any objections. "We'll take that, Captain."

"Good. Calothrick, see Mr. Bogunheim about a bunk. He's our third mate. We set sail tomorrow morning."

We signed the logbook and we were ready to go.

The *Lunglance* was a typical member of her breed, the dustwhaling trimaran. She was one hundred and five feet long, ninety feet at the beam. She was constructed almost

33

entirely of metal, as Nullaqua has no wood. Her three metallic hulls were kept constantly gleaming by the abrasive action of the Sea of Dust. She had four masts and a dizzying number of sails: topsails, topgallant sails, fore-royals, mainsails, and mizzens, twenty sails in all. Her deck was covered by a kind of plastic processed from grease and crushed whalebone; otherwise, the pitiless Nullaquan sun would have made the deck too hot to stand on. The crew slept in airtight, filter-equipped whalehide tents, lashed to the deck through great iron rings and bolts.

Captain Desperandum slept in his cabin belowdecks at the stern; I slept near the bow in the kitchen, next door to the ship's stores. Both compartments were shielded from the dust by electrostatic fields across the hatches. The fields were powered by a small generator located in the middle hull; it ran on whale oil.

There were twenty-five men aboard: myself, the cook; Captain Desperandum and his three mates, Flack, Grent, and Bogunheim; two coopers, two blacksmiths, our cabin boy, Meggle, and fifteen regular seamen. All but Calothrick were squat Nullaquans with hairy noses and a dreadful anonymity of feature.

And then there was our lookout, the surgically altered alien woman, Dalusa. I will have much to say of her, later.

Chapter 3

A Conversation with the Lookout

We set sail at dawn, bound south-southeast for the krill grounds near the Seagull Peninsula. Breakfast was gruel, requiring little effort on my part; the captain and his mates ate muffins and kippered octopi.

The men ate on deck in a long galley tent. Even without his mask the Nullaquan sailor is unusually terse while at sea. I saw that Calothrick had painted his mask during the night; he now had an electric blue lightning bolt on each cheek. It was unique. No native Nullaquan had ever seen a lightning bolt.

After some thought I settled on a large broken heart as my own motif.

Lunch proved more difficult. My predecessor had left me battered utensils, great pots and tubs of dubious cleanliness, and a cupboard full of unmarked Nullaquan spices. I pride myself on my control of the gastronomic art, but these primitive conditions hampered me.

I had young Meggle, the cabin boy, clean the pots while I sampled the spices. One had a sharp metallic taste reminiscent of rusty iron; the second was vaguely like horseradish; a third was analogous to mustard but with a bitter aftertaste. The fourth was salt. I never found out what the fifth was. A single whiff convinced me that it had spoiled.

I dragged a barrel of hardtack from the ship's stores next door and managed to make it palatable. It was an epic task, but I was rewarded by the single-minded attention paid by the whalers to their food. Without their masks they all looked the same. They were so quiet, except for the occasional belch, that I wondered if they were planning a mutiny.

They seemed a surly lot. All wore drab brown or blue bellbottom trousers and corduroy shirts. Their arms were tanned, their faces pale, with faint seams along the sides where their dustmasks adhered. Six of the men had shaved a narrow band along their temples, around their heads, and across their jaws to get a better seal. To a man, the crew was bedecked with Aspect necklaces, thin metal chains from which dangled one or more symbols of the fragments of God, for, according to the odd Nullaquan creed, the most any man could expect was the attention of a minor fraction of the Deity. Growth, Luck, Love, Dominance, the usual sailor's Aspects were all represented, some also on rings and bracelets. The jewelry was not considered magical in itself, but merely served as a focal point for prayer. Although I was not religious, I myself owned a platinum Creation ring; it was an artist's Aspect.

The men ate mechanically, their faces impassive, as if they were unused to expressing emotion, or as if the pale faces were only another kind of mask, held on with invisible straps.

They ate at a long plastic-topped table, bolted to the deck. Another table stood at its head at the end of the galley tent, like the cap to a T. It held food. There was just enough room between the two tables for the men to pick up plastic plates and serve themselves.

Calothrick, tired of the monotonous working of jaws, tried to start a conversation with the grizzled veteran at his right. "Fine weather today," he said.

All the men stopped eating. Forks in hands, they stared at the unfortunate Calothrick, giving him the clinical interest that a doctor might give to a boil. Finally, concluding from his embarrassed silence that he had nothing more to say, they continued eating.

It was an unfortunate conversational gambit, anyway. There was no weather in Nullaqua. Only climate.

My first meeting with the alien woman, Dalusa, came at the last meal of the day. The sun had already sunk beyond the western rim of the Nullaqua Crater, and evening was lit by the dust-filtered roseate glow reflected from the cliffs four hundred miles to the east. I was working in the kitchen when she came through the hatch.

Dalusa was five feet tall. Black, fur-covered batwings furled around her, attached to bony struts that were elongated metacarpals and phalanges. She had ten fingers on each hand; five supported the wing, the others were free, much like a human hand, even to red lacquer on the fingernails. Her arms were of unusual length; they would have hung to her knees if she had not habitually carried them bent at the elbows, her hands in front of her breast.

I felt an instant's bewilderment, unable to tell if she were a bat altered to look like a woman, or a woman attempting bathood.

Dalusa's face had a refined, sculpted beauty that could only have come from surgical alteration. An artist had weilded the scalpels.

She wore a loose, extremely lightweight white robe, actually just an opaque film that hung from her muscular shoulders and pectorals down to her knees. There was something subtly wrong with her legs. There was a list, almost a waddle, in her walk. It seemed obvious that she had been born with legs radically different from the mock-human ones now supporting her.

Dalusa had shoulder-length black hair with the same dull sheen as the velvety fur on her wings.

She spoke. Her voice was a low, liquid baritone, so astonishing in its subtle tonal variation from common humanity that I almost missed the words.

"Are you the cook?"

"Yes, madam," I said belatedly. "John Newhouse, late of Venice, Earth. What can I do for you?"

"Jonnuhaus?" she repeated, blinking.

"Yes."

"My name is Dalusa, I am the lookout. Would you like to shake my hand?"

I shook her hand. Her grip was weak, and her hand was unusually hot, though not damp. Apparently her body temperature was a few degrees higher than a human being's.

"Do you talk?" she said. "That's nice. None of the sailors will say anything to me, their custom, I think. I believe they think I am bad luck."

"How short-sighted of them," I said.

"And Captain Desperandum is very single-minded. Did you say you were from Earth?"

"Yes."

"That is humanity's birthplace, isn't it? You and I will have to talk about that sometime. I'm very interested in that. But I'm taking up your time. I came to say that I am authorized to prepare my own meals. I'm afraid I'll have to take up some of the space in your kitchen."

"Perhaps you dislike the style of my cooking. I know other styles."

"Oh no, oh no, it's not that. It's just that there are trace elements . . . and I have allergies to proteins in your food. And then there are bacteria. I have to take a lot of precautions."

"You'll be in here often then."

"Yes. I keep all my food in that box." With her unnaturally elongated arm, she pointed at a blue metal-bound chest. It was under an iron table that was bolted to the kitchen floor.

I checked a half-dozen bubbling cobblers in the stove while tha alien woman dragged her box out and opened it. She appropriated a brass pot and sprayed the inside with an all-purpose antibiotic aerosol.

"Is this your first whaling voyage?" I asked.

She emptied a half-dozen biscuitlike discs of meat into the pot, sprinkled spice over them, and set the pot on the whale-oil flame. I pumped the hand primer a few times to make sure it would burn evenly.

"Oh no. This is my third trip with Captain Desperandum. This voyage I should have enough money saved to leave the planet."

"Are you eager to leave?"

"Very much eager."

"Why did you come here in the first place?"

"Friends brought me. At least I thought they were my friends. But they left me here. . . . I didn't understand them. Maybe I couldn't."

A faintly acrid whiff of frying alien meat came from the stove. "A basic psychological dichotomy," I hazarded.

"No. I'm sure that can't be it. No, it was worse with my own people. I never fitten in, was never accepted. I was never *kikiye*'." Her altered mouth moved awkwardly to form the word.

"So you had yourself changed."

"You object?"

"Not at all. So you were left here, you needed money, you signed up with Desperandum?"

"That's so." She took a flexible metal spatula out of a drawer, sprayed it with the aerosol, and turned over the slices of meat. "No one else would have me."

"But Desperandum doesn't go by the book."

"Yes. He is an alien, of course, and he is also very old. I think."

That was bad news. There was no telling what bizarre behavior I might see from Desperandum. Men grow tricky, motives strange, when the subconscious lust for death turns traitor.

"He seems a decent sort," I said. I smiled. "At least he showed considerable taste in hiring you."

"You are kind." She took a dirty plate off the stand, scrubbed it with coarse sand, and sterilized it. She took the pot off the fire and stabbed a piece of meat with a long fork. "Do you mind if I eat here?"

"No. Why?"

"The man in the galley tent don't like it when I eat with them."

"I should think you'd be a great favorite."

She put down her fork. "Mr. Jonnuhaus—"

"John."

"John, I show you something."

She held out here right hand. I looked at it. A prickly red rash spread across her thin dactylate fingers. I reached for her arm. "You've burned yourself."

"No! Don't touch me." She leapt back, unfurling her wings with a rustle. A faint puff of air crossed my face. "Do you see, you shook my hand. Your hand was damp, a

39

little, and there are enzymes, oils, microorganisms. I have allergies, John."

"I hurt you."

"It's nothing. It will go away in an hour. But can you see now, why the sailors? . . . I can never touch anyone. Or allow anyone to touch me."

I was silent for a few moments. "That's a misfortune," I said. At the sight of the rash a strange sickish feeling spread through me, that doubled and trebled as I heard her explanation.

She refurled her wings so that they hung in neat togalike folds, and drew herself stiffly to her full height. "I know that when a man and woman touch each other it leads to other things. Those things would kill me."

The sickness spread. I felt a little weak. I had felt no real attraction to the bat-woman when I first saw her, but at the news of her inaccessibility I felt a sudden lurch of desire.

"I understand," I said.

"I had to tell you that, John, but I hope we'll be good friends, anyway."

"I see no obstacles to that," I said carefully.

She smiled. Then she picked a slice of meat from her plate with her red-lacquered fingernails and, daintily, ate it.

Chapter 4

A Strange Revelation

On the fourth day of our voyage I made an odd discovery. It happened while I was searching the ship's hold for something to stimulate my rather discriminating palate. I was testing an ale barrel with my seaman's jackknife, when the tip of the blade snapped off and the knife flew from my hand. I was searching for it in the dimness of a corner of the hold when I noticed a hairline crack in the bulkhead. It was the joint of a camouflaged door. My curiousity was aroused. The door had a lock, which I quickly picked; I then discovered that the *Lunglance* had a false compartment. Inside the cramped, alcove were several dissassembled pieces of an engine, complete with batteries; a propeller blade; two large tanks of oxygen; and a tub of glue. The glue was an extremely strong adhesive. I found my jackknife and dipped a blade into the stuff. I had to tug to get it back out. I resealed the tub, closed the hidden door, went up on deck, and threw the knife overboard. It was impossible to get the glue off it, and it would have betrayed my knowledge of the secret.

Because of its position at the bottom of a pit, the Sea of Dust has longer nights than days. That night I had a long time to puzzle over my discovery. The propeller especially perplexed me. They are never used at sea because they stir up dust clouds.

I was sure of one thing. Only Captain Desperandum could be responsible for the hidden alcove, as only he could have ordered the alterations done. Most whaling captains were responsible to a shore-based firm, but Desperandum owned the *Lunglance* outright.

Nor was this the end of our captain's oddities. On the next morning Desperandum suddenly ordered all sails furled and the *Lunglance* stopped dead in the dust.

Desparandum emerged from his cabin carrying at least three hundred pounds of high-test fishing line. The deck creaked under his weight, as he himself weighed easily over four hundred pounds. Producing a hook the size of my arm, he baited it with a chunk of shark meat and threw it overboard. He turn returned to his cabin and demanded breakfast. I quickly obliged. He ate, sent his mates out, and then called me into the cabin.

Desparandum's cabin was spartanly furnished; a custommade bunk six feet long and five feet wide, a massive metal swivel chair, a work table that folded down from a wall. Detail maps of Nullaqua, hand drawn on cheap, yellowing graph paper, were stuck to the walls with poster wax. In the glass-fronted cabinet to my right were several pickled specimens of Nullaquan fauna, trapped in specimen jars. The stuffed head of a large carnivorous fish, mounted on a metal plaque, had been bolted to the stern wall. Its jaws gaped wide to reveal discolored, serrated teeth. Below were thick glass windows, giving a view of the placid, gray, dust sea. The western rim of the crater loomed on the horizon, glowing in the sunlight like a massive crescent moon.

"Newhouse," the captain said, seating himself with a creak in his swivel chair, "You're from Earth. You know what science is." Desperandum's voice was low and raspy.

"Yes, sir," I said. "And I have the highest respect for the Academy."

"The Academy." Desperandum bristled. "You err, Newhouse, and err badly, when you associate real science with that superannuated group of fools. What can you expect from men who have to spend three hundred years just to obtain a doctorate?"

"Yes, sir," I said, testing him. "Old people do tend to get set in their ways sometimes."

"True!" he said. Desperandum was deeper than he looked. "I'm a scientist," he said. "No doctorate, maybe, a

42

false name, perhaps, but that's neither here nor there. I'm here to find out something, and when I aim to find out I don't let anything stand in my way. Do you realize just how little is really known about this planet? Or about this ocean?"

"Men have lived here for five hundred years, Captain."

"Five hundred years of imbeciles, Newhouse. Have a seat. Let's talk man to man." He waved one meaty hand, speckled with blond hairs, at a metal bench by the door. I sat.

"All the major questions about Nullaqua are still unanswered. The first survey teams—with Academy support, mind you—took some samples, declared the place fit for humanity, and left. Answer me this, Newhouse. Why does everything alive here have water in its tissues, even though it never rains?"

I reviewed my memories of the books I had read before moving to Nullaqua. "Well, I've heard it said that there's a sort of sludgy substrata, deep beneath the surface . . . something about aquatic toadstools that float to the surface to spawn. They burst open and plankton absorbs the water."

"Not a bad theory," said Desperandum judiciously. "I want to be the first to prove it. Understand now, I have no objections to making a profit. You'll get your share of a successful voyage, just like everyone else."

"I was never in any fear of that, Captain."

"But there are lots of little questions that nag at my mind. What causes currents in the dust? How deep is it? What lives down there, what kinds of scavengers? How do they find their food without sight or echo location? How do they breathe? It's the very opacity of the sea that infuriates, that bothers me, Newhouse. I can't *see* into it.

"And another thing. We know that the place was inhabitable when the Elder Culture was here. Why did they build outposts on the airless surface?"

"I don't know," I said facetiously. "Maybe they were afraid of something."

"I'm not," Desperandum said. "But then there's the crew to think about. They can't possibly understand what I'm doing; they never have. You're closer to them than I am; if they start to get restless, tell me about it. I'll see to it that there's a bonus for you when the cruise is done."

"You can depend on me, Captain," I said, humoring him. "You might consider young Calothrick, too. He's from off world and he's closer to the crew than I am."

Desperandum's broad flat forehead creased as he thought about it. "No," he said finally. "I don't like him. Don't trust him. There's something greasy about him."

That surprised me. Calothrick greasy? I made a mental note to check on him. Perhaps he was having withdrawal symptoms.

Desperandum continued, "Thanks for the suggestion, anyway. Dismissed. Oh, by the way, birdfish casserole for lunch."

"Aye aye, sir." I left.

How odd, I thought. Why did Desperandum bother with a dead end like science?

My reverie was interrupted by a shout from Flack, the first mate. Captain Desperandum had hooked something.

Desperandum padded eagerly from his cabin. He had attached the end of the fishline to a stout winch and he immediately ordered it reeled in. His impatience was marvelous and two of the crew began cranking the winch at a tremendous rate.

In and in they reeled. Suddenly the fish broke the surface and exploded. The rapid change in pressure had been too much for it.

Crestfallen, Desperandum examined the rags of fish left on the hook. Small shiny fish nibbled at the remnants that had been scattered for yards in all directions. There was just enough of a ruptured head on the hook to suggest that the creature was blind. There was no hint as to how it breathed in the airless depths. Perhaps it breathed silicon.

Desperandum tried again. He rebaited the hook with the head of his new catch and dropped it overboard. Two new crewmembers took the windlass and began unreeling the line. Down it went, a hundred yards, two hundred, three hundred, four hundred.

Suddenly something took the hook and the windlass began unreeling at an insane speed, nearly fracturing the arm of one of the sailors. No one dared to set the catch that would stop the windlass; it might have taken his fingers off.

"Cut! Cut!" said the second mate.

"Ceramic fiber!" shouted Desperandum over the whir of the windlass. "It'll hold it!"

Abruptly we were out of line. The entire ship lurched, the deck tilted crazily, and with a terrific screech the windlass was ripped free of the deck, snapping some bolts and ripping others right up through the metal. In a flash, the windlass vanished beneath the surface.

Thoughtfully, Desperandum leaned on the collapsible rail and watched the dust swirl where the windlass had gone down. Then he turned to stare at the whaling hoists attached to the masts, as if he thought them admirable deepsea fishing tackle. I saw several crew members exchange significant glances. Then Desperadum returned to his cabin. In a moment came the order to set sail again.

The two blacksmiths produced their hammers and welding equipment and repaired the holes in the deck that the bolts had made when they pulled through.

I was about to return to the kitchen when a sudden shadow flickered across the deck in front of me. I glanced up and was shocked to see some kind of winged monster sliding and darting through the air. It stopped, fluttered, and settled neatly inside the crow's nest. It was Dalusa.

There came a coded series of blasts from the horns in the crow's nest. On her scouting flight the lookout woman had seen a dustwhale, two miles to starboard. Desperandum was out on deck at once. At his orders, the *Lunglance* turned into the wind, in the position known as all aback. Then the foresail lines were rapidly hauled through their winches so that the foresails were almost perpendicular to the wind. For a moment the clew lines hung slack; then the sails filled with a muffled snap and the ship heeled onto a starboard tack. The foresails were straightened and the *Lunglance* moved sluggishly forward. The *Lunglance* always moved sluggishly. She was not built for speed, and there was little chance of wind with any force in the 500-mile Nullaqua Crater.

Soon the whale was in sight. As the ship crept up on the

lethargic beast, three of the seamen opened veins in their elbows and collected blood in a beaker. Blackburn, our harpooneer, took the beaker and poured the blood into the central chamber of his piston-equipped harpoon with its four shiny barbed vanes. Then he walked nonchalantly to the starboard harpoon gun and loaded it. There was enough blood left for two extra harpoons if need be.

It was odd, but convenient, that human blood should be a lethal poison to the dustwhale. But it was no odder than the whale's production of Flare. Like all good things, syncophine in sufficient quantity is a lethal poison.

We sailed closer to the creature, and it grew larger and larger. It seemed that no living creature had a right to be that huge.

Suddenly there was a loud *chunk* sound from the starboard. The vast bulk in the distance suddenly sprouted a harpoon. The silence was broken by a shrill scream. It was the whale.

The beast, bewildered, began to swim toward us. Blackburn took the opportunity to sink a second and a third poisoned harpoon into its vast, armored back. With a final frightened squeal the creature sounded, only a few yards from our bow. It was under for less than a minute; then it floated to the surface, dead.

The dustwhale was a vast flounderlike creature, seventy-five feet long and perhaps thirty feet across. The largest part of its body was its mouth, a huge crevasse bristling with tough baleen. It had teeth in its throat to crush the hard-shelled Nullaquan plankton. It used the large amount of silicon it ingested in this way to build a tough black armor, jointed by strips of gray whaleskin. Such armor is tough, but flexible; if it were rigid, the dustwhale would be forced to molt when it grew. This gave the whale an odd sort of hexagon checkerboard pattern of black and gray on its entire body. One could tell a whale's age by counting the growth rings on an armor plate. The rings were not very well defined, since Nullaqua has no seasons and the food supply is constant. But they were there, and it was seldom that one found a whale more than fifty years old. Like all Nullaquan surface fish, the dustwhale is air-breathing and cold-blooded. Dustwhales often travel in pods.

We cruised to the side of the dead monster. Six crewmen, one of them Calothrick, leapt off the ship onto the creature's back, carrying huge hooks attached to metal cables.

The lookout honked her horn twice, sharply. This was the warning signal for sharks. A coded blast off the smaller horn gave their position: three points off the port bow.

Mr. Grent, the second mate, was overseeing the loading operation. He grew agitated and the crew began to jump frantically, imbedding their hooks as deeply as possible into the flesh of the monster. It was best to snag a rib.

I had heard much about the Nullaquan shark, so I walked across the deck to see their approach. What a disappointment! Advancing from the west was a small flock of flying fish, their jewellike chitinous wings flashing green in the sunlight. Were these the legendary carnivores, these fluttery creatures little larger than earthly goldfish? But then perhaps there were vast numbers of them, with small, but sharp teeth and a total disregard for their own preservation. . . .

Then I saw fins split the surface beneath the flying fish and a half-dozen shiny black bodies surged through the dust like advancing torpedoes. It was startling, almost macabre, to see the bulbous tip of each black fin suddenly open to reveal a large, staring blue eye!

So, then the flying fish were only pilot fish, leading the sharks to slaughter in exchange for tidbits. With their wings they could go much higher and see much farther than the dust-bound sharks.

Suddenly the third mate, Mr. Bogunheim, thrust a long whaling spade into my hand and yelled at me to help repel the creatures. Nothing loath, I ran across the deck to the rail to join the rest of the crew.

The sharks were already attacking. The dust roiled like lava, and thick gouts of purplish liquid burst from the lacerated body of the whale. The sailors had finished imbedding their hooks, and they jumped to the relative safety of the deck. There came a loud clanking and clattering from the hoists and triple tackle as the whale was slowly, slowly, hauled on board. The ship began to list. I stabbed downward into the thrashing mass of sharks and felt my spade bite flesh. A sailor moaned through his mask as one of the pilot fish flew on deck and bit him stingingly on the calf. Those fish were small but they had sharp teeth. They fluttered on board to harass the sailors, fell to the deck, then scuttled overboard on their stiff wings like so many monster ants.

I stopped my attack on the sharks for a moment to stamp on a flying fish. Suddenly the whaling spade was almost wrenched from my grasp. Startled, I pulled up a five-foot metal stub, bitten clean through. I was taken aback. Then I saw a pilot fish flap toward me. Swinging my stub like a bat, I sent it splattered back into the sea.

Suddenly a swift shape, borne aloft on crooked batwings, swooped past the edge of the ship. It was Dalusa, dragging a metal-mesh net. The fluttering group of pilot fish stopped harassing the crew and quickly sought the safety of the sea.

The crew moved out of the way as the hoisted whale slowly settled onto the deck. The *Lunglance* listed and thick purplish blood ran out under the rail and into the sea. One shark, more voracious than the rest, leapt onto the deck after its vanished prey. Flopping and snapping it bit out a final oozing chunk of meat and then rolled overboard again.

The sharks milled indecisively in the bloody dust. Then they towed their dead comrades out of spade range, devoured them in a leisurely manner, and swam languidly away.

The crew settled down to the task of butchering the whale. First, the armored skin was peeled off in strips and soaked in a copper tub with a chemical that made it more pliable. Then the meat was efficiently sliced off with spades and axes. Piece by piece, it was fed into a clanking hand-powered grinder and processed for oil and water. Our two coopers sawed through the broad, stavelike ribs and began to machine them into ivory barrels. The smaller ribs and a few of the vertebrae were taken for scrimshaw.

Under the pretense of getting whale steaks I shoved a

few pounds of the intestine into an iron bucket and hid it in the kitchen.

The crew shoved the remaining offal overboard with shovels and tough metal-bristled pushbrooms. I looked over the side. At the touch of moisture, the parched dust had clumped into a slate gray, doughy mass. Soon, I knew, the crystalline spores of Nullaquan plankton would sense the presence of water and begin to grow, soaking up all the moisture through their tiny pores and biochemically altering the dust into a transparent micalike shell. A strange world, I thought, where a man could lean over the rail and spit emeralds.

A crude but satisfactory method of extracting syncophine was through processing with ethyl alcohol. So, when the crew celebrated that night, I appropriated a few pints of strong ale and started work.

The process was about half done when I heard a quick triple rap on the hatch. I took the brew off the range and put it in the oven, then went up the stairs and opened the hatch. It was Calothrick.

"Holy Death," he said profanely, walking down the stairs and pulling off his lightning-striped dustmask. There were red indentations from the seal of the dustmask on his temples and across his sparsely stubbled cheeks. "I can't stand that beer." He sniffed at the air, then grinned.

"Knew I could depend on you, John," he said happily. He zipped open his sailor's tunic and pulled out a flattened plastic pouch from an inside pocket. There were a few drops of syncophine in one corner.

"I've been saving up," he said. "Y'want a quick blast?"

"Why not?" I said. Calothrick pulled his eyedropper out of his belt.

"I've been meaning to come down here and talk," he said. "You've got it pretty soft down here. You don't have to associate with that stinking crowd of sailors. What a bunch of stooges! I don't think they know how to talk. I mean, like you or me." He handed me the eyedropper. "Here, you can go first."

I looked at the massive dose of syncophine he had given

me through a misplaced sense of generosity. "I'd better sit down for this," I said.

Calothrick winked. "Been a while, huh? Boy, the days sure crawl by without it."

I opened my mouth and squeezed five drops of Flare out onto my tongue. A metallic-tasting numbness spread through my mouth. My eyes began to water. I handed the dropper back to Calothrick. He shook his bag a few times, then sucked out an even larger dose than he had given me. Suddenly my vision blurred. I closed my eyes.

"Here's greasy luck," said Calothrick cheerfully, giving the dustwhaler's traditional toast. His voice sounded unnaturally loud. Unconsciously I gripped the seat of my stool.

There was a sudden icy tingling at the base of my spine. Abruptly an overwhelming rush like channelized lightning rocketed up my spine to burst inside my skull. I felt it distinctly. The top of my skull lifted neatly off, and a cold blue flame shot through the center of my head. My eyes shocked open and the flame settled down to an even, steady burning, like the flare of a welding torch. The stove, the unwashed utensils, Calothrick's ecstatic face, everything had an unnatural shininess to it, as if every object were suddenly venting energy from some internal reservoir. Electric blue dots and lozenges floated at the edges of my vision. I looked at my hands. I, too, was glowing.

"How long?" Calothrick said suddenly.

"How long till what?"

"How long till you can distill some Flare that's fit to do up?"

"I don't know," I said with difficulty. "I can finish distilling by tomorrow night if I work at it. But I don't know how good it'll be. I won't know its strength."

"Oh, I'm not afraid of its being *too strong*," said Calothrick. He giggled.

I thought about the potful of whale intestine slowly growing cold in the unlit oven. I felt disinclined to get up and put it back on the stove. It seemed like an immense effort, obviously beyond my capabilities.

"What were we talking about?" Calothrick asked.

I hesitated. "About how strong it was."

"Yeah, yeah, I remember."

"One of us will have to try it out first," I said. "There might be impurities. Maybe dangerous. You want to draw straws?"

"Dangerous," muttered Calothrick. He seemed troubled. Then he smiled. "Did I tell you about that man, the one who's been pestering me all the time?"

"No. Are you being mistreated? Have you told the mates about it?"

"No, it's not that, it's this kid named Murphig. A Nullaquan. It's his first time out and he keeps asking me questions, you know, about where I'm from and what I'm doing out here. A real nuisance. I mean, I'm not too good at lying."

An odd statement, that last one, I thought. If it were a lie, it was very much a lie, because he had told it with an aura of perfect innocence and truth.

"So?" I said.

"So, he's about your build, you know? You've seen him, the one with green and white target shapes on his cheeks?"

"Yes."

"Well, why not try it out on him?"

I thought it over. "You want me to put *Flare* in his *food*?"

"Why not?" Calothrick demanded. "I'll do it if you don't have the—if you don't want to."

The Flare was beginning to wear off. "Yeah, you do it," I said. I rubbed my left eye, the one with the grayish dead spot; it was beginning to ache. I got up off the stool, took the pot out of the oven, and put it back on the range. I turned on the heat.

"Pump that primer a few times, will you Dumonty," I said tiredly.

"Monty," he corrected, pumping. "Say, you got lots in there. That'll keep 'em happy back in the Highisle, huh?"

"Yeah, sure," I said. But my erstwhile roommates on Piety Street had burned me, maneuvered me, made me their pawn. I was not interested in vengeance of course;

51

that was beneath me. Only simple justice. There would indeed be a large quantity of syncophine, even after I had finished the distilling process. But they would never see any of it. I had already settled that.

Calothrick might object. But I would deal with him later.

Chapter 5

The Lie

"Tell me about Earth," Dalusa said.

"All right." How many times had I told the lie and to how many women? I had lost count. Over twenty years ago the inspired falsehood had sprung like a full-blown rose into my mind, watered by panic, fertilized by youthful romanticism. I had feigned reluctance countless times; countless times my youthful brow was knit with a counterfeit pain from counterfeit memories. But for Dalusa it was different, Dalusa deserved better. I resolved to lie my hardest for her.

"I can't tell you of the whole planet," I said, picking my words with care. "Only the few acres, here and there, that chance allowed me to know. Thirty-four years ago I was born in Venice, an ancient city, once a nation. It was built on an island, and called the Bride of the Sea. Venice was surrounded by an arm of the World Ocean, a great salt sea called the Middle of the World. As a child I would watch the sea, watch foamy waves batter the shore, and tease my eyes with the scattered gleaming of the sun on the water's choppy surface. It seemed that the ocean went on forever, engulfing the planet like a second atmosphere. There is enough water in Earth's blue and bitter seas to drown the Sea of Dust some thirty times over.

"But about Venice. Imagine a glorious golden city, so old that it is betrayed by the very rocks beneath it. A city once marvellous and proud, glittering, beautiful, holding the slowly gathered loot of the seven seas. There was no navy like the Venetian Navy, no art like her art, no rulers like her doges. Venice was queen among the cities of Italia and Bohemia, like a great diamond among sapphires. Of Earth's cities Venice was the first to reach for the stars. Of course, Venice was founded long before man knew flight, but Venetian genius turned the long dream into reality. Wooden birds, hatched from the brain of the immortal Leonardo da Venice, sculled through the Venetian skies, carrying the city's red and silver banners. . . .

"But the land began to falter. Little was thought of it at first. There were many to propose solutions, much wealth with which to carry them out. Dike off the sea? No, Venice is surrounded by mudflats. Perhaps float the island itself? But nature responded with fire and earthquake to any such attempt. The rock beneath the city was unstable, rotten with caverns, seething with subtle molten fires. The risk of a cataclysm was too great.

"The decline was slow; many times there were eras of relative stability, when citizens looked at one another and saw the despair slowly melting away. But no sooner was there a renewal of confidence, than there would be another slow shock, a dull descent. Then her husband betrayed the Bride of the Sea.

"By my own time, the Venetians lived in the third and second stories of buildings partially drowned. The population was less than a tenth of that in Venice's heyday. Mine was a remnant of an ancient, noble family. I remember my childhood well. I spent much time poling or paddling my dead black pagoda through the sunken streets. The water was still and clear and always cold. I remember the sunken, shattered pylons, the drowned statues festooned with anemones, sea urchins crawling spinily across the drowned mosaic faces of Venetian madonnas, obscured by scattered sand. Sometimes I dived in the cold water, seeking treasure, and would come home clammy and slimed with weed, to meet my mother's mild and sad rebuke . . ." here my voice broke momentarily. My mother had died when I was young; surely it still hurt somewhere inside. And this was my own life, my own lie, a surrogate of my own grafted to my personality. It was flowing tonight as never before, even though I had to give it the elaborate, involuted verbal style

54

favored by Terrans. My own creation, my own lie, my own soul. My art. Tears came to my eyes.

"It was a restrictive culture, stylized past all vitality, still beautiful, like the perfectly preserved cadaver of a young bride. And I was essentially alone. Many times I would leave parties or poetry contests to wander the streets alone in my black pagoda. Many of the Venetian buildings were deserted, theaters, mansions, pensions crumbling in wet decay. I didn't mind a little mildew, and I often climbed through empty windows and waded across slimy floors with my lantern. I would sometimes collect odd shells—"

"What?'" Dalusa said.

"Shells. The exoskeletons of dead aquatic organisms. Sometimes I found the barnacled remnants of earlier centuries. The shard of a Greek amphora, a shiny aluminum can from the Industrial Age, some washed-up fragment of a lost memory . . ."

"Why did you leave?"

"I grew older. There was talk of marriage, of an alliance to an ancient family even more decrepit than our own. I knew suddenly that I could not endure another week in Venice, not another day of their gentle melancholy, not another hour of fashionable despair. I might have fled to another city. Paris, Portland, Angkor Wat . . . but one planet seemed too small. I left and have not seen Venice since. Nor do I care to see it."

My voice shook. This hurt me, bit clear to the bone. This invented history was much closer to me than my actual childhood, those sordid years of rejection and scorn only partially cushioned by my father's ill-gotten wealth. I had tried to forget my boorish idiot comrades, my father's muscular attempts to force me into his own mold, and the breakdowns. The breakdowns that had revealed to me the miracle of tranquilizers. Then stimulants, first legitimately, then a whole illicit galaxy of multicolored pills, encapsulated joy. Instant strength, sniffed, swallowed, inhaled, or injected. I had tried to forget the pain and had partially succeeded. But I treasured the memories of those drugs. I knew I had finally found a career I could stomach. Within a few years I was dealing, a respected member of an odd, but profitable, sub branch of pharmacy. I had never regretted it.

Later I fell asleep.

* * *

The next morning the sailors were unusually voluble. One of the largest, one Perkum by name, paused in mid-chew to remark, "You know, this captain of ours is really a nut!"

The others nodded and went back to their meal.

Captain Desperandum was everywhere that day, taking dust samples with hinged buckets, dissecting a dead pilot fish, taking notes on the behavior of the sharks. In full view of the crew he took my sheared-off whaling spade and bent it double with his bare hands. Seeing this the crew returned to their tasks with redoubled vigor.

By midmorning we had reached the fringes of the krill soals. Desperandum threw a seine behind the ship and dragged out several hundred pounds of plankton. It scattered across the deck like so many pounds of jewels, nugget-sized organisms in every conceivable geometric shape: pyramids, tetrahedrons, octahedrons, even dodecahedrons, glittering in their silicon armor and crunching into green smears beneath the captain's boots.

At noon we found another whale, ploughing sluggishly through the dust and chewing plankton with a noise like grinding pack ice. Three new crewmembers went through the bloodletting ritual. Blackburn returned to his harpoon gun and, surprisingly, missed with the first harpoon. The second and third lodged, though, and as the ship drew nearer he fired a fourth at almost point-blank range, piercing the creature's lungs so that it choked and spurted purplish blood. It died in convulsions.

Dalusa swept in from the airborne archimedean spiral that was her scouting pattern. Sharks were approaching at top speed from the south, but they were two miles away. There was plenty of time to butcher the whale; the sharks would be too late to get more than the leavings. I wondered how they knew of the whale's death at all. Had the flying fish spotted the monster from the air? Or was there a subtler method?

To the south loomed the massive moon-colored wall of the Nullaqua Crater specifically, the monstrous jutting of the Seagull Peninsula.

There was a thick white band about a quarter of the way up the peninsular cliffside. I knew intellectually that the band was actually two stacked miles of white seagulls, nesting, screaming, and squabbling in incredible numbers. Survival was strictly defined for the seagulls; at the bottom, they would be smothered by plummeting guano, at the top, they would starve to death commuting to and from their nests. Beneath the white band it was greenish gray, where tenacious lichen struggled desperately for survival, clinging to centuries' accumulated layers of parched excrement.

Somewhere in that immense gray band was a small dung-covered lump that was the Highislite warship *Progress*. It was a quarter of a mile up the cliff, tossed to destruction by the dust tsunami of the Glimmer Catastrophe, three centuries ago. For decades the wreck had been visible, its gleaming mangled metal a memento mori, a symbol of guilt to generations of Nullaquans. For years a pair of binoculars could pick out the crushed mummies that were the *Progress's* crew, perfectly preserved, their yawning mouths with blackened tongues, slowly packing full of dry gray guano. Ton after ton of raining birdshit slowly buried the wreck, clinging like ice to the tangled rigging, dripping across the metal hull like gray stalactites. Now the wreck was completely shrouded, dotted with lichen, buried by time like a childhood aspiration never attained or an unhappy love affair slowly smoothed over by the amassed trivia of day-to-day living. It was a final end to the Nullaquan Civil War, and the supposed punishment for sin had resulted in a crushing moral victory for the slaughtered Perseverans, fanatic fundamentalists of the worst stripe. It was true that they had been butchered to a man a year before the catastrophe but even so, after three centuries their dead hands were still locked around Nullaqua's living throat.

I knew all this intellectually, but to the eye, it was only a cliff with a white band and a green band.

I saw a sudden green flash of wings in the distance. The sharks were coming.

I sensed someone looming at my right shoulder. I turned.

Suddenly I was staring directly into a pair of eyes, dark eyes, much like my own, eyes framed by the plastic lenses of a dustmask that was decorated with green and white target shapes. The man, Murphig, was exactly my height. The whole contact lasted only a second. Then, uncomfortably, we both turned to watch the advance of the sharks. They were closing rapidly. I shuddered. I was not sure why; it wasn't the sharks.

Surprisingly, the sharks and their winged comrades declined to attack the crew. Instead they slashed sullenly at the floating, dust-caked intestines that we had thrown overboard. With more-than-beastlike sagacity, they knew that the whale had already been processed. There could be no profit in aggression. Still, they stayed out of range of our whaling spades.

I returned to the kitchen and began to run my brew through a crude but efficient still I had jury-rigged out of some loose copper tubing. At lunch I explained plausibly to Dalusa that it was a still and I planned to make brandy. She immediately lost interest; alcohol had no appeal for her.

I finished before supper with a little less than an ounce of watery black fluid. The black-market Flare I had refined from pure Nullaquan gut oil was almost transparent. I wondered if I should try straining the new brew.

Supper was uneventful. I piled the unbreakable dishes into a large coarse-woven sack and carried them into the kitchen. I found Dalusa there. Spread on the cabinet before her was a large Nullaquan seagull, dead. Pale purple fluid leaked from a triple puncture in its breast. Dalusa was staring at the dead bird in rapt fascination, her own wings furled, her hands clasped before her breast.

I walked heavily down the stairs, but she showed no sign of realizing my presence. I looked at the bird. It had a wingspan of about four feet; its yellow eyes, glazed and dead, were half veiled by lids that moved from the bottom of the eye upward. Its beak was lined with tiny conical teeth.

Its feet were strangest, long black weblike nets, weighted at the bottom with nodules of bone. Obviously its fishing pattern was to swoop above the opaque dust and net blindly for whatever might be below the surface.

I loomed at Dalusa's shoulder. She did not look up, but continued to stare at the bird. A thick drop of lavender blood oozed slowly across one of its breast feathers and dripped onto the cabinet top. There was no remorse in the lookout's face, only absorption, mixed with an emotion I could not name. Perhaps no human could.

"Dalusa," I said softly.

She jumped, half unfurling her wings; it was the inborn reflex of any flying creature. Her feet clicked when they touched the deck again. I looked down. She was wearing a whalehide sandal arrangement on each foot; straps crossed her instep and looped around the outside of her heel. Curling upward from the base of the toes on each foot were three stainless steel hooks, six inches long and barbed. Artificial claws.

"You've been hunting," I observed.

"Yes."

"And you caught this bird."

"Yes."

"Are you going to eat it?"

"Eat it?" she repeated blankly. She looked at me in confusion. She was adorable. I felt a sudden strong sadistic urge to kiss her.

I restrained myself. "You're wearing claws," I said.

"Yes!" she said, almost defiantly. "We all had them, in the old days." Silence. "Did you know, did I tell you, I was there when your people met mine for the first time?"

I blinked. "A scientific expedition?"

"Yes, they said so."

"Sponsored by the Academy, no doubt," I told myself aloud.

"What?"

"Nothing. What happened then?"

"They talked to us," Dalusa said. She ran one pale fingertip along the wing of the bird, slowly. "How beautifully they spoke. From my place in the shadows my heart went out to them. How wise they were. How graceful in the way they *walked,* always touching the ground. They were so solid and stable. But the elders listened and were angry. They swooped on them from above and tore the humans, ripped them to tatters with their claws. I could do nothing, me, only a child and not *kikiye'*. I could only love them and cry by myself in the darkness. But even their blood was beautiful, rich and red, like flower petals. Not like this thing's . . ."

There was a triple rap on the hatch. Calothrick. "Come in," I shouted, and Calothrick entered, pulling off his mask. He stopped dead when he saw Dalusa.

"You have things to discuss," she said suddenly. She pulled open the oven, snatched a pair of insulated potholders off two hooks on the side of a cupboard, and pulled out a covered dish. "I will go eat with the sailors."

"No, stay," I said. She stopped for a second, then glanced at me with such an intensity of emotion that I was taken aback. "We will talk later tonight." She picked up her mask from the table, a china white mask with a single blood red teardrop from the corner of the right eye. She started up the stairs; Calothrick, coming down, gave her a wide berth. She left; the hatch snapped shut.

"Weird," opined Calothrick, shaking his head. Wisps of tangled blond hair fell over his eyes. He brushed them aside with one hand. His fingernails were dirty. "Say . . . you're not carrying on with that, um—" he searched for a noun and couldn't find it. "—with her, are you?"

"Yes and no," I said. "I might if there were any point to it. But there isn't."

"With that?" said Calothrick incredulously. He seemed more shrill than usual. I looked at him closely. Sure enough, the whites of his eyes were tinged slightly yellow with Flare withdrawal. He was suffering. "What about Millicent?"

"Yes, of course, there's always her," I lied smoothly.

After the way she betrayed me I wouldn't have touched her with an electric prod. "But after all, what is love but an emotional obsession . . ."

"Caused by sexual deprivation, yeah, I know that one," Calothrick said. "But that bat-woman gives me the creeps. She looks all right, but it's all surgery, y'know? I mean, if it weren't for the scalpel she'd have big ears and claws and fangs. She has her own tent, y'know. The men say she sleeps upside down. Hangs by her toes from the ridgepole."

I was annoyed. "Mmm," I said. I changed the subject. "What do you think of the behavior of those sharks?"

"Sharks? I dunno. Murphig was talking to me about them just a while back. He spends a lot of his time *watching* things, just sort of *looking* at them. He says they can smell death at a distance. Maybe, he says, smell it before it happens. The kid's as nuts as Desperandum. Yeah, and speaking of Murphig . . . how's the stuff coming?"

I swung open a cabinet door and took out a metal bottle. In the bottom was a thin scum of syncophine. "Terrific," said Calothrick, sniffing the bottle. He pulled his plastic packet out of his shirt and poured in a thin rivulet of the brew. "Ugh. It's black," he commented, sealing the bag. "First thing tomorrow, then, Murphig gets it."

"Not too much," I said. "It could be extremely powerful stuff."

"Yeah, yeah, right, I'll be careful," Calothrick said impatiently. "Oh, by the way, d'you see that plankton out there tonight? Quite a sight." He strapped his mask back on, slipped the Flare inside his shirt and went up through the hatch.

I sat down on the kitchen stool and began to clean out the still, meticulously. Sooner or later I would have to brew some spirits with it, if only to divert any possible suspicions of Dalusa's. I wondered about my attraction to the woman. There were mixed motives, I decided.

Not least of which were the amplified joys to be derived from her company. It may seem strange to you, reader, but put yourself in my place. Did your mistress, lover, companion, ever lean forward to breathe hotly on your neck? Do you remember the quasi-erotic shiver it sent down your spine? Then imagine a like stimulus from Dalusa, whose body temperature exceeded that of a human being. Remember the contagious excitement received when your partner's heartbeat grows more rapid? Dalusa's was almost twice that of a normal woman. If the idea of woman as an object of mystery appeals to you, well, Dalusa's alien origin gave her a permanent romantic shroud. And she was beautiful. What matter if her classic loveliness was the gift of surgery? Surely you agree that it is the soul inside that we love, rather than the mere exterior. You agree with it, whether you believe it or not.

That was the major facet of the attraction. But there was a strong subliminal one, that Dalusa had perhaps deliberately fostered.

All of us have sadomasochistic qualities. Mine, though well controlled, seemed strong. I had admitted to myself long ago that my use of drugs was killing me. The whole concept had become only another part of my self-image. But cruelty to oneself is the first and most crucial step in cruelty to others.

I thought it all out and it all bored me. I decided to go on deck and see the plankton Calothrick had mentioned. I put on my dustmask.

As I stepped up through the hatch, the last sunbeams slipped upward off the eastern lip of the Nullaqua Crater. It was night.

Yet there were stars, and a dim green glow arose from the sea around us. I walked to the rail and saw that all around the *Lunglance* were square miles of krill, burning with bioluminescence. It was magnificent. Suddenly I smiled inside my mask. I was glad I had done the things that had brought me to this spot. I was glad to be alive, since I needed life to see this.

As I leaned over the rail a dark, winged shape flitted quickly before me and a narrow, dark swath opened in the closely packed crystals. A glowing bundle of them moved outward and upward with a swallow's grace, then, suddenly, was directly over me. Green coals cascaded around me, falling like nuggets of lava from a cool volcano, scattering and pattering across the deck.

The hair on the back of my neck was stirred by the wind from her wings as Dalusa settled beside me. A weblike black net was still strapped to one of her ankles.

She had brought me jewels in the seagull's severed foot.

Chapter 6
The Storm

Next morning at breakfast Calothrick sat next to Murphig at the table in the dining tent. Palming his dropper, he squeezed a massive dose of the brew into Murphig's gruel. Then he caught my eye and winked.

We both examined Murphig anxiously. Stolidly, the young Nullaquan cleaned his bowl, rose with perfect composure, and walked out of the tent. I had always known syncophine to have a powerful and rapid effect, but I kept an eye on him for a full hour anyway. Nothing. Obviously it was still much too weak.

When we killed our next whale I appropriated two buckets of intestines and started work. Calothrick met me after lunch that day and we had a hurried consultation.

"Still too weak," I said. "Maybe there's a certain organ that yields the Flare. The spleen maybe, the pancreas . . ."

"Spleen my eye," said Calothrick testily. He was always on edge now, his eyeballs were yellowed and bloodshot. "What the death good will that do us? Neither one of us knows anything about anatomy, much less a whale's. They probably don't even *have* spleens."

"We'll just have to do what we can," I said patiently. "Sooner or later we'll get it right. You want to try out some of the brew? Maybe there's something physically abnormal about Murphig."

"Why torture me?" Calothrick said savagely. "We've fed it to him for four days now, stronger every time, and nothing. Nothing! Y'know, I'm starting to wonder about you. You're taking it mighty easily; you're as cool as a fish. No trembling, no jitters. Maybe you've got something I don't know about. Like a bottle."

"Really," I chided.

"You got it soft, you know? You stay down here where it's cool, serving that slop you call food—Don't you shush me, man! You know what I have to go through up there? They order me around like a dog, tell me to do things I obviously never heard of before, and I can't even ask a question, man. Not with that mask on! If I want to ask something, I'd have to take it off and bloody my lungs with raw air. Every speck of dust is just like a needle inside your chest. No way! You realize that there are seven different kinds of ropes on this tub? And that doesn't count the halliards, the braces, the downhauls *or* the clew lines. And there's twenty sails on this thing! Uppers and lowers and mizzens and gallants . . . how am I supposed to get 'em straight? So they send me to do the shit jobs. The stuff nobody else will touch. Look at this hand!"

Calothrick thrust his hand in front of my face. He had barked three of his knuckles. His fingers trembled noticeably. "I had to overhaul the secondary generator this morning. I did all the work while Grent stood by cleaning his fingernails and telling me what to do. And this afternoon I start work on the sewage recycler. No water for a bath. Hardly enough to wipe off with a sponge every other day! No, we save every drop. And down in the hold we have dozens of barrels full of cool, clean water. 'Bound for the Highisle,' they say. Shipowners wallow in luxury while we cook on deck."

"You volunteered," I said pointedly.

"Don't remind me."

"And you're not the only green hand on board."

"Murphig was born here, man. It makes all the difference. Anyway, I'll take care of Murphig in my own way."

"Cheer up," I said flatly. "I'll have the new brew ready by tonight. Half a bottle full. That'll do it if anything will."

Calothrick stared sullenly at me for a few seconds, then went back on deck.

Human blood poisoned whales, I told myself. I wondered if Calothrick would poison the sharks if I kicked him overboard.

That night Calothrick met me in the kitchen just before supper. "Have you got it ready?" he said, slapping his dust-mask down on the counter.

"Yeah," I said, "but I've been thinking. It's odd. After all, Nullaquans have been here for five hundred years. You'd think that everyone would be doing Flare by now. Or at least know about it."

"So? Let's go, you're wasting time."

I was annoyed. "Wait a minute, hear me out," I said calmly. "I'm not sure you know this, but the first settlers on Nullaqua were a very small group. Only about fifty."

"What in Oblivion's name are you talking about?" Calothrick had a flair for Nullaquan profanity.

"Keep listening. They cloned off the first generation, you see, to fit in with Nullaquan conditions. Hairy noses, thick eyelids, the whole thing, you understand? There were no direct descendants of the original fifty. They'd all had themselves sterilized. So, maybe, in all that genetic manipulation, there was a gene that causes immunity to Flare."

"Immunity?" said Calothrick aghast.

"Why not? I suppose it's possible. The founders were opposed to unorthodox drugs in general. Death, they probably knew about Flare from the beginning. They were cranks, but they weren't stupid."

"You mean we fed that bastard a whole bottle of Flare for nothing?" Calothrick said. He had turned pale.

"I'm sure of it. I'm not a geneticist."

"Give me the bottle," Calothrick said flatly.

I did. "What I said about it's being dangerous still holds, of course."

"Shut up." Calothrick pulled his eyedropper out, tilted the bottle, and sucked up a minimal dose. "I suppose I'm an idiot to do this."

"You said it, not me."

"On the other hand . . . well, here's greasy luck." Calothrick squeezed out a shot onto his tongue. He swallowed.

We waited. "Any effect?" I said finally.

Calothrick opened his mouth, but choked on words. Finally he emitted a strangled, "Wow!"

"If it's that good I think I'll have a small blast myself. Lend me your dropper." I plucked it out of his nerveless fingers. Ideally I should have waited to see if Calothrick suffered any adverse side effects, but I was hurting. Besides, it seemed to have done him a world of good. A blasted grin was plastered on his face and the yellow withdrawal tinge was already fading from his eyes. I sucked up a normal dose and swallowed.

By the time I got up from the floor, the food had grown cold and I had to reheat it. But it had been worth it.

I felt reasonably content about the bottle. There was a good five months' worth in it for one man, maybe two months for Calothrick and me. Calothrick was something of an enthusiast.

I hid the bottle in the cupboard. At night, after the washing up was done, or rather scrubbing up—I used sand, not water, I wrestled with my self-control about a second dose. I almost always limited myself to one a day, less than that most of the time. Or at least a great deal of the time. Sometimes I even quit for two or three weeks at a stretch. But my alcohol intake went up sharply then, and, coming from a frontier planet like Bunyan, I knew the debilitating and addictive effects of booze. I wasn't sure about the long-term effects of Flare. But better an unknown devil than one known only too well, I thought. Besides, this new discovery called for a celebration. Abstinence was ridiculous.

I took my eyedropper from its hiding place under the counter and measured off a healthy dose—perhaps more then healthy. I turned off the lights in the kitchen, laid down on my pallet, pulled the quilt up to my chin, and took the blast. I had just enough time to put the dropper under my pillow before the rush hit me.

Hallucinations filled the darkness. Electric blue networks expanded across my field of vision. They were replaced by glittering silver dots, linked in inextricable, inexplicable geometric patterns. Bright energy surged up my spine. I felt that my brain was dissolving."

Someone stepped over me. A sudden conviction overcame me—it was the Angel of Death. I felt sudden panic. I fought it down, repeating internal mantras: Tranquillity. Peace. Calm. Repose. . . .

The same someone pulled open the cupboard. The click as it opened was as loud as a gunshot. Aural hallucinations now, echoes, alien voices speaking. I struggled to get a grip on myself. Someone was definitely in the room. I tried to pull myself up on one elbow; dizziness overcame me. I sank back onto the pillow, grinning helplessly.

"Who is it?" I tried to say, but the words came out sounding like "wizard." A bad omen. I was helpless.

I heard the distorted thuds of feet on the steps. The hatch snapped open. It shut again.

I suddenly realized that it must have been Calothrick who had come down for another dose and been unwilling to wake me. The image of Calothrick appeared in my mind's eye, recognizably him, although his narrow head was adorned with bulbous gray spines. Calothrick, of course. Nothing to worry about. I fell asleep.

Next morning I discovered that my bottle was gone. Calothrick and I argued, he holding forth the absurd theory that I had hidden it for my own use, myself convinced that he had squirreled it away somewhere else on board. The third possibility, that someone else had lifted it, aroused mutual apprehension. Since there was nothing we could do about it, we resolved to keep our eyes open and hope for the best.

The *Lunglance* could have stayed by the Seagull Peninsula until she had filled her holds. But too many planets had been raped and made worthless for mankind to indulge in this kind of exploitation any more. We did not stop; we were bound on the Grand Tour, to sail the entirety of the Sea of Dust on the slow, circular winds.

Nullaqua's weather patterns were peculiar. There was a very slight temperature differential between the middle of the Nullaqua Crater, located on the equator, and the upper and lower margins. This was enough to power a weak double convection cell. Heated air rose from the equator and diverged northward and southward. Traveling, it cooled, to sweep slowly downward along the cliffsides and back to the equator. Though most of the dust had precipitated out of it, there were still enough microscopic rock grains to chew slowly away at the base of the cliff. Over the eons the base was slowly eaten away; eventually, the top of the cliff, weakened, would shelve off and crumble downward. Then there would be a pile of rubble at sea level to protect the cliff from further damage. Ages would pass before the wind could get at the cliff again. And it was never strong.

Or almost never. My first hint that it might be otherwise came when I was awakened one morning, six weeks into our cruise, by a loud series of blasts from the lookout's horn. I did not recognize the code; it is one infrequently used.

Captain Desperandum emerged from his cabin, looked to the southeast, and immediately ordered all the sails furled. I followed his gaze. I saw a mighty gray wall; behind it was the shadowed backdrop of the Nullaqua Crater. A minor island, I thought. We must have drifted toward it during the night.

No. Even as I watched, the wall grew longer. The crew ran up the ratlines and began to tug at the sails. I looked up. There was a man in the lookout's nest; Dalusa was nowhere in sight. Anxiety struck me.

The tents were folded quickly and stowed belowdecks. All loose objects were tied down or taken below. Mr. Bogunheim had a single word for me in response to my gestured queries. "Storm," he said.

Sailors were already deserting the deck, leaping quickly through the hatches. I went below with them. Tramping through the kitchen, they went through the door into the storeroom. Other crew members were already there, sitting glumly on barrels and lighting up their rank pipes. Calothrick leaned against the false bulkhead, slipping his eyedropper back into his belt. Seeing me, he burst into a series of uncontrollable giggles.

Dalusa was not there. I rushed past the startled second mate, ripped open the hatch, and jumped up on deck. Shrugging, Grent slammed the hatch behind me. There was no sense in getting us all killed.

The deck seemed deserted. Then I spotted Desperandum

standing beside the hatch that led to his cabin, notebook in hand. He was staring at the storm front with a critical eye. His mask was cream colored and haphazardly marked with mathematical symbols in blue.

"Fascinating, isn't it?" he offered. His gravelly bass came tinnily through the mask's speaker.

I flapped my arms. Desperandum stared at me nonplussed. Then comprehension dawned. "The lookout. Isn't she down in the storeroom with the others?"

I shook my head. "Well, she's not with me," Desperandum said. "She must still be out on her morning scouting trip. That's a shame. She was quite a help to us." He shook his head regretfully. "Bad luck. These things don't happen often. Freak wind conditions, or perhaps seismic disturbance. They say there's a heat vent in the far edge of that bay, the one the storm came from. We'll just have to weather this out, I suppose. Let's go down to the cabin. Come along now; we don't want to lose you, too." Desperandum took my wrist casually. His grip was as secure as steel manacles.

We went down to his cabin together. Desperandum pulled off his mask and ran one hand over his short-cropped reddish blond hair. He glanced at the thick glass windows in the back of the cabin and clicked his tongue regretfully. "Those windows," he said. "And after all the trouble I went through getting them installed. When the dust blast gets through with them they'll be opaque. Useless."

I was in an agony to get back on deck. So psychotically strong was my urge to aid Dalusa that I was unable even to stop and rationally consider my motives. I pulled off my mask with an elaborate charade of casualness, but Desperandum, his insights into human behavior sharpened by hundreds of years of experience, saw through me. "You're agitated," he said. "Try to calm yourself. There were a few things about Dalusa that I think you ought to know—"

"Look!" I shouted. "Isn't that she, outside the window?"

The response to a cry like that is automatic. As Desperandum turned, I pulled on my mask and leapt up the stairs and through the hatch. Desperandum's shout was cut off

70

short as I slammed it behind me. I hoped he would have more sense than to come up on deck after me.

But I reckoned without a captain's devotion to his men. The hatch slammed open and I barely had time to flatten myself behind a try-pot before Desperandum leapt up onto the deck. He glanced around quickly for a few seconds, saw the approaching storm, and leapt back down into his cabin. The hatch was slammed and locked.

There was no lightning, no thunder. The wind was dead calm. I stared in fascination at the approaching wall. It was not as solid as it appeared at a distance; horizontal flattened strata of wind-driven dust sleeted out before the storm's main front, and long curls and involutions reached out like gaseous tentacles before expanding into nothingness. The light dimmed, and the morning sun was already obscured by an encroaching gust. Adrenalin poured into my bloodstream. Already my overly vivid imagination was hard at work; I had a sudden vision of the ruthless sandblast stripping away my skin, blasting my mask's plastic lenses into a frosted blur, abrading my tough rubbery mask into useless shreds, scouring my face away with a million crystalline impacts. In seconds I would be lacerated into a gooey skeletal framework, my bones stripped clean, cut thinner and thinner by the merciless gusts and finally annihilated. A total panic rush stung me; I leapt up from behind the try-pots and ran across the deck.

Then I saw a winged blur silhouetted against the approaching wall. Wind puffed past me, sharpened particles stung my exposed hands and throat. The light was going out. Dalusa was out of control, blowing like a leaf, almost pinwheeling. She was going to cross the *Lunglance*'s bow. Now I could hear a dim roar as I ran across the plastic-clad deck. A strong gust struck the stern and the *Lunglance*'s wire braces sang like violin strings. Another gust stung me and almost knocked me off my feet, but I scrambled to the bow. I was in time. But Dalusa was too high, flying out of my reach—no, she swooped downward. But was it far enough?

Then, as she passed, I jumped overboard. And, to my own surprise, I caught her legs in a panic grip. We hit the

71

dust and went under, but only for a second. Its specific gravity was higher than that of water and we floated like corks. I grabbed Dalusa's dust-caked hair and struck out for the space between the *Lunglance*'s middle and port hulls.

I tried to draw a breath and started to strangle. Dust had completely plugged my mask filters. With an immense effort of will, I stopped my frantic inhalation and breathed outward sharply. My ears popped, but the filters cleared.

Dalusa was choking, clawing at her mask with sharp red fingernails. Whacking the back of my head against the center hull, I loomed out of the dust and struck her sharply with the side of my clenched fist, into the solar plexus. Dust spurted out of the end of her mask filter and she drew in a shuddery breath.

She threw her arms convulsively around my neck and dust gritted against my skin. I was completely coated with the floury stuff; it adhered tenaciously to the thin layer of human oils and greases on my skin. No chance of contamination now.

Then the wind rose to a howl and the sky was completely obscured. It was as black as pitch underneath the *Lunglance*. Dalusa's long arms had a startling panic strength; it was obvious that she had no idea of how to swim. I tried to give her a reassuring pat on the back, but her wings were in the way. At last I reached clumsily over her arms—a difficult task, since her velvety but tough wings almost completely enshrouded me—and patted her between the shoulder blades. Her grip loosened a fraction.

The wind was beginning to push the *Lunglance* slowly through the dust. That was bad. If the ship ever turned her stern or her bow to face the wind, the gale would sweep along between the hulls and kill us.

I stopped treading dust and trudgeon kicked twice in order to float on my back. I braced both feet against the center hull, holding Dalusa almost completely out of the dust. She let go of my neck, lying quietly at full length on top of me. The buoyancy of the dust was enough to hold the round breathing filter of my mask out into the air, but the rest of my head was submerged. Most of Dalusa's weight was concentrated in her massive flying muscles.

Then she slid grittily downward along my torso and rested her masked cheek against my chest. My face floated up out of the dust. Some of Dalusa's body heat was beginning to conduct itself through the layers of dust that separated us. If I started to sweat at the areas of contact she would contract a severe rash. I exhaled sharply and sank a little under her so that fresh dust could adhere to me.

Feeling me sink, Dalusa linked her arms loosely around my waist. It was still pitch black. I knew her position only by touch. There was no sound but the hollow roar of the wind and the gritty sandpaper sound that the dust made as it rasped at the *Lunglance* above us.

But we were safe, at least for the moment. My heartbeat had slowed now and I became aware of the definite eroticism of the situation. I lifted my dustcaked arms and put my hands over Dalusa's shoulder blades. The muscles under my fingers grew stiff, then relaxed and moved. Her cheek still rested on my chest, but, suddenly, I became aware that she had reached down and was caressing the backs of my calves. Her arms were longer than I had realized; I felt a sudden chill, not unmixed with lust, at the realization of Dalusa's essential alienness.

She continued to stroke the backs of my legs. It was not a particularly sensual feeling in itself; the dust was gritty on my skin, and my loose sailor's bellbottoms were bunched uncomfortably around my knees. But the idea of it was startlingly provocative. So abstracted was the relationship between us that any physical contact, however minor, assumed fantastic, grotesque importance. I stroked Dalusa's back with my dry, gritty hands. I hesitated about embracing her. The sensation of having her wings pinioned might make her panic.

We lay there for several minutes, listening to the wind moan and savoring our comfortless contact. I could feel Dalusa's heart beating with amphetaminelike speed against my chest. Then, amazingly, her hands began to creep upward along the insides of my legs, inside my baggy trousers. Inch by inch they slid across my skin, triggering reac-

73

tions that were frightening in their intensity. There was an almost sinister quality to it, afloat in the dust on my back in the dark, while Dalusa's feverishly hot fingers grittily caressed the insides of my thighs. My own heart was thudding now, and my hands were limp on Dalusa's back.

Then Dalusa's hands stopped and squeezed. Suddenly a series of quick spasms went through me, so bewildering in their intensity that I had difficulty identifying them as sexual. At the same time Dalusa shuddered against me. Drained, we relaxed against each other. I think I slept.

At any rate, I suddenly became aware of the glare of the sun on the dust outside. Dalusa lay unmoving on my chest. Pushing off gently from the central hull, I began to backstroke out from the *Lunglance*'s shadow.

When the sunlight hit us, Dalusa stirred. Flexing her wings, she knelt on my torso and flapped into the air, shaking dust from the fur on her wings and from her streaming hair. I swam to the ship's port side, and, kicking violently, was just able to reach up and grab the edge of the deck. It was metal smooth; all the plastic had been blasted off by the storm. Hoisting myself up, I grabbed the bottom rung of the guard rail. It screeched in protest at my weight. The upper rail had been weakened by the wind. When I grabbed it, it broke in my hand and cut the edge of my palm. Dust soaked up the blood that trickled down my wrist. As soon as I recovered my breath, for the sudden fall had slammed me bruisingly into the *Lunglance*'s hull, I pulled myself up with a mask-muffled groan and slid under the railing. I found a new ship. She was clean, incredibly clean, as clean as a picked bone. Several braces had snapped, eaten in two by the awful friction of the wind. The masts gleamed. Every surface was smooth and shiny; I could see my masked reflection on the deck where the sand had eaten down into the bare metal. I looked like the ghost of some humanoid alien, so completely was I covered with the pallid dust. It shook itself loose from my clothing with every step. The plastic had been completely stripped from the deck, except in the thin shadow zones behind the masts, try-pots, and starboard railing. When the sun came fully overhead, the glare would be blinding.

The hatch to the kitchen creaked open; I froze. The first mate, Mr. Flack, came cautiously out and looked at the clear skies. Then he looked back down the hatch and nodded.

Turning, he saw me standing completely still in the middle of the barren metal deck. He, too, froze. I envisioned the thoughts going through his head: *Good Lord! Look at the poor bastard. His skin's been completely stripped off and replaced with dust, he's been mummified alive. I hope he didn't suffer much.*

Then he said, "Get below and clean up, Newhouse. The men'll be eating soon."

I stood by the hatch while the crew tramped past me up the stairs. Calothrick was last; when he emerged, he gave me an overly jovial whack on the shoulder that raised a cloud of dust.

I went through the electrostatic field inside the hatch and it ripped a great sheet of dust off my skin and a cloud out of my hair. As I walked down the stairs a torrent of loosened dust poured out of the bottom of my trousers and out from under my shirt. Still wearing the dustmask, I stripped and whacked my clothing against the counter top. Dust flew. I took off the mask, sneezed, and put it back on. I would have to wait for the stuff to settle before I tried to clean it up. I went to the cistern, twisted the tap, and soaked up a spongeful of water. Its contact against my skin was sybaritic in its luxury.

I pulled a change of clothes out of my duffel bag and took the broom out of its closet. The dust was so light and frictionless that it was almost impossible to pick up, and my energetic attempts only reopened the cut on the side of my hand. A drop of blood slid slowly down the edge of my wrist.

Then Dalusa came down the hatch.

"How are you? Are you all right?" she said. I smiled at her show of anxiety.

"I'm fine," I said. "A few abrasions, and I bruised myself getting back on board. Oh, and I cut my hand a little." I held up the injury.

"Au' " Dalusa said, stepping closer to me. "You're *bleeding.*"

"It's nothing," I said. She was staring at the small wound with all the rapt fascination that a mantis shows at the appearance of a fly. "How are you?" I asked lamely.

"Fine. I was flying at the same speed as the dust, it wasn't able to hurt me. But it ruined my dress. See?"

It was true. The thin white film had grown dingy; millions of microscopic particles had somehow imbedded themselves in its polymerized surface.

"Maybe you can wash it," I said.

"Oh, no need. I have yards and yards of material. I'll make another one."

An uncomfortable silence fell. I put down the broom and dabbed at the cut with my sponge. It would clot soon.

"When we were under the ship, John . . ."

"Yes."

"I liked what we did."

Our eyes met. Perhaps, if she had been a normal woman, and I a normal man, we would have understood one another then. Poets say that souls meet and touch with the eyes as their medium. But even within the same species, what man can claim to really know a woman's mind? Her next words were barely audible.

"Did you?"

"Very much."

"I want you to kiss me, John." She stepped closer yet, so close that I could feel the radiant heat of her body.

"You know I can't do that."

She closed her eyes and tilted her chin upward. I put my hands behind my back. "It'll hurt you," I said, weakening. Her perfectly sculptured lips parted a fraction of an inch.

I leaned forward and, with the care of a biologist dissecting a unique specimen, touched my mouth to hers. She responded with dreamy hunger, and the whole situation took on an aspect of glazed unreality. A chill swept through me. The silken, almost molten fusion of textures and pressures was like the culmination of a murder. Tears came to my eyes as her tongue slid across the atrociously sensitive ridges of my upper palate, just behind my teeth. I responded. Her own teeth were abnormally sharp, and there was a subtle alien tang in the taste of her mouth, unlike any human woman's. Breath hissed from her nostrils and warmed my cheek.

At last we broke. Already her lips were puffing, swelling, growing sticky and inflamed before my eyes. The seconds seemed to ooze by, moving as slowly as bubbles rising upward through sludge. Dalusa said nothing, but tears welled from the corners of her eyes and slid thinly down her cheeks and across her swollen mouth.

I raised my injured hand and held it before her face. Then I clenched my fist and squeezed. The half-formed scab parted stickily and a fresh drop of blood oozed slowly down my wrist. We stood unmoving there and watched each other hurt.

Chapter 7

Arnar

The *Lunglance* needed docking and repair. Captain Desperandum set sail for the Pentacle Islands. Nullaqua's third-largest settlement, Arnar, was built on the largest of these islands.

It took us three days to limp into harbor. After telephoning several shipbuilding companies and arranging things to his satisfaction, Desperandum assembled the crew and granted shore leave to the lot of us. He himself stayed on board.

The men tramped down the gangplank and across the dented metal docks to one of the massive elevators on the Arnar cliffside. The huge cubicle ran on charged metal rails to the city above us. The men filed glumly into the elevator and shut the guard railing behind them. I was with them; so was Calothrick. Dalusa was nowhere in sight; probably, she was riding the thermals upward to the city. I had not talked to Dalusa in the past three days. She had moved some of her concentrated food out of the kitchen and retired to her tent on deck. I had gone to speak to her, but she had kept her mask on when I walked into her tent. It was impossible to carry on even a onesided conversation when she faced me with the china white mask, its one blood red teardrop under the right eye providing a grotesque counterpoint. Perhaps she was regretting her action, perhaps she was ill from the aftereffects of the kiss, probably both. I refused to bother her.

The second mate punched the activating button and the elevator began to climb sluggishly up the side of the cliff.

The docks, whalers, and merchant vessels below us shrank slowly; the air was gradually clearing, so that from my position at the rail I could look down on a thin grayish haze blanketing the surface of the Sea of Dust. The opposite rim of the Nullaqua Crater shone in the distance, as small as I had ever seen it, but more sharply delineated now that we were above the haze. It eclipsed only six degrees of the western horizon. It was hard to realize that the rim was a sloping series of cliffs, seventy miles high; it looked more like an encroaching storm front, gray thunderheads looming across the sky. Still, that was enough to give one the gnawing feeling that one was living in a bowl. To the east, behind us, the cliffs of the eastern rim covered almost half the sky. Morning came at noon at the base of the cliffs. It was the gleam of the western cliffs, towering out of the atmosphere and reflecting the raw sunlight with moonlike intensity, that lit the early part of the day.

The air was still clearing, taking on the merciless cloudless clarity of all Nullaqua's island cities. I dared to take off my mask and sniff at the air. It was clean. I took in a deep lungful and turned to speak to Calothrick.

All the sailors were staring at me, standing stolid, sullen, and forbidding, as if I had committed some breach of etiquette. I put my mask back on.

At last the elevator reached the top of the cliff and clicked to a stop in front of a broad metal aisle, fenced on the cliffside with a woven-wire fence seven feet high. This assured that not even the drunkest Nullaquan sailor could stumble off the cliff and squander his bodily fluids on the rocks far below. The second mate grabbed the elevator guardrail and swung it open with a creak. I got ready to step off the elevator.

Suddenly the sailors rushed forward in a body, surprising me and bouncing me off the woven-wire fence with a rattle.

I stumbled after them and found that we were on Starcross Street, the heart of Arnàr's red-light district. Both sides of the broad avenue were lined with bars, nightclubs, wrestling auditoriums, mechanized amusement parlors, and houses of ill repute.

Suddenly Flack ripped off his checkered mask and emitted an ear-splitting whoop. As if on signal, the rest of the sailors pulled off their masks and clipped them onto rings on the sides of their belts. Meanwhile Flack had launched into an elaborate spiel, delivered at the top of his lungs:

"I'm Flack, the first mate of the *Lunglance,* the finest ship in the fleet!"

The rest of the sailors whooped in agreement.

"I'm tough as spring steel and as tall as the mainmast! I leave footsteps in concrete and crack rocks with my fists! I can kill a flying fish by looking at it and bite a shark to death in a fair fight! Harpoons are my toothpicks and I clean my nails with jackhammers!"

Flack put his hands on his hips and did a quick jig step, then leapt into the air and clicked his heels together three times before landing. The *Lunglance*'s crew burst into frenzied applause. Already a crowd was gathering, mostly garishly dressed Nullaquan "daisies" and their pimps. There were also upwards of a dozen hairy-nosed Nullaquan urchins and several rival sailors, easily spotted by their tanned arms and pale faces.

Now Grent was starting his speech. "Stand back, stand back, give me room to strut, or I'll make room over your massacred bodies! Don't tangle with *me,* I'm way out of your league! I can stick my arm in the ocean and fish pebbles off the bottom! Don't try me, don't try me or I'll kick down the Nullaqua Wall and spill out all your air! I can tie a knot in a mainmast with one hand, my breath melts sheet steel. . . ."

Seeing that this was likely to go on for some time, I tugged on Calothrick's sleeve and we slipped unobtrusively out of the crowd and up the street.

"Hey, wow, you want a quick blast? Let's go up that alley," Calothrick said, pulling his eyedropper out of his belt. I followed him into the dim shade cast by the wall of a tattoo parlor. With a grin, Calothrick pulled his plastic packet out of his shirt and slurped up a frightening dose of Flare. He handed me the eyedropper.

"Monty, I can't use this much," I said.

"Aw, death, John, that's no dose for a red-blooded man like yourself," Calothrick protested. He took the dropper out of my fingers, tilted his head back, and squirted the entire dose down his throat. "See?" He put his dropper back into the packet and slurped up another massive overdose.

"I'm cutting down." I said. "We have to save all we can for the folks back at the New House."

"Aw, there'll be plenty. How many more whales are we going to kill, anyway? Twenty? Thirty? You could have gallons of the stuff by the time we get back. Sure you don't want a shot?"

"Not one that size."

"Suit yourself," Calothrick shrugged, and swallowed a second massive dose.

"You must have diluted it," I concluded suddenly. Taking the packet out of his limp fingers, I helped myself to a quarter of a dropperful. "Here's to Ericald Svobold," I said. "May he rest in the peace he deserves."

"Who?"

"Ericald Svobold. He was the discoverer of Flare. That's what they tell me anyway."

I swallowed the dose. The reaction was instant and powerful; a blue electric rush leapt up my spine and turned my carefully organized neuronic circuitry into a random, chaotic mass of sparkings and fusings. Like Calothrick, I leaned against the wall, grinning helplessly.

A voice sounded close to my ear. "Are you good-natured, darlin'?"

I quickly slipped the Flare packet inside my shirt and attempted to rally my scattered faculties. "What?"

A middle-aged Nullaquan daisy, her face decorated with a thin scattering of multicolored powder on her cheekbones, had appeared in the alley during my incapacitation. "You lookin' for a good time, sailor?"

"I, uh, I don't . . ."

"I think I need to lie down," Calothrick mumbled, slumped against the wall.

The daisy helped him to his feet. "Come along, darlin'. I know just the place for you." She pulled his arm over her hefty shoulders, reaching behind him to pat his wallet with maternal fingers. She winked at me; to my Flare-scorched

81

mind her face seemed glazed and intolerably bright. "Goodbye and greasy luck, whaler. Drop by Madam Annie's some time. Ask for Melda."

It was an enormous relief to have them both gone. I leaned against the wall and drew in a long, cool breath. Things seemed to sort themselves out, and a buried memory gnawed at my subconscious. An errand . . . oh yes, the brandy.

I walked with excessive care out into the street and stepped onto a narrow, sluggish slidewalk. At length I slid by a bar that looked slightly less sleazy than most and stepped off the walk. Foot-high block letters, painted with greenish enamel that contained the bioluminescent juices of Nullaquan plankton, read "Merkle's Bar and Grill."

I walked inside and put one foot on the brass rail at the bottom of the bar. Merkle, a squat, balding man with a tanned face and braided nose mustachios, appeared before me.

"What'll it be, sailor?"

"Give me a shot of old redeye," I growled in authentic sailor fashion.

"What the hell's that?"

I explained. "Sorry, you won't find any of that here," Merkle said virtuously. "Nothing stronger than twenty proof."

"Why not?"

"Because it's illegal."

Surely I might have known. "Give me an ale," I said. Even the relative mildness of the drinks was not enough to force a determined Nullaquan sailor into a state of sobriety. I was sluicing the taste of Flare from the back of my throat when I heard a sudden bellowing outbreak of hostility from the denizens at the end of the bar. There was a clank and a slosh as someone dented a metal tankard of beer against someone else's head. It was followed by the quick meaty rap of knuckles on teeth.

"We'll have none of that," roared Merkle, picking up a long aluminum cudgel dotted with brass studs. "Go outside and settle your differences like gentlemen."

"I'll break his teeth in," promised one of the combatants,

draining the remnants of the beer in the dented tankard. Leaning across the bar and staring past the line of pale, inebriated sailors' faces, I recognized Blackburn, the *Lunglance*'s harpooneer. He and his opponent, a brawny Nullaquan whose nosehair was inextricably mingled with a large red mustache, walked out underneath a hanging whale-oil lamp.

I finished the ale. Scooping up a tip left for a waitress on a nearby round, plastic-topped table, I paid for the drink.

"Do you deliver?" I asked.

"Yeah, sure do, sailor."

I ordered three quarts of the strongest ale he had delivered down to the *Lunglance* and wrote our dock address on a plastic pad. Then I left.

Outside, Blackburn and his acquaintance were still at it. I shouldered my way through the crowd that had gathered and watched them shoving and squirming on the pavement. The hair in one of Blackburn's nostrils was soaked and dripping with blood; his opponent had a split lip. Unable to regain their feet, they were raining blows on one-another's midsections. Their punches were growing weaker and weaker, but since both men were also weakening, the blows had about the same effect as before. With every knuckly impact they opened their mouths and bawled, short basso profundo howls cut off by gasping intakes of air.

Finally, bruised and wheezing, they clung helplessly to one another, pulling in deep, quavery, achy breaths.

Slowly, with agonizing attention, the red-mustached sailor clenched his fist. Blackburn weakly lifted one hand. "To death with this," he said through puffed lips. "Let's get up off the street and go get laid."

"Yeah," said the other, nodding. Mumbles of disappointment arose from the crowd as the two shakily helped one another to their feet and stumbled arm in arm to a cheery bordello just across the street.

It was time for lunch, I concluded, glancing up at the sun. I took the slidewalk up off Starcross Street into a more respectable part of town, where I stopped at a small outdoor restaurant and indulged myself with a beefsteak. It was not up to par; the Nullaquan spices added in its preparation gave the juices a thin acid sting, and the salad that accompanied it had been assembled with startling incompetence. I left without tipping and decided to go back to the *Lunglance* to check on Dalusa.

My progress was impeded slightly by a massive brawl on Starcross Street. Several *Lunglance* crewmembers were involved, and if they had seen me they would probably have insisted that I join in. I took a detour through Tailor Street. Perhaps that avenue had once been occupied by tailors, but if so, they had been displaced by mask salesmen. Store after store was open, their windows stocked with an amazing variety of paints. I still had some left over in my duffel bag, from when I had bought my mask in the Highisle. It seemed like years ago. It was only two months.

Remembering the elevator's irritatingly slow crawl up the Arnarian cliffside, I expected a similar long wait to reach the docks below. Imagine my suprise when the machine fell so swiftly that my feet were actually floating several inches above the elevator floor. My companions in the elevator already had their masks on; they floated as solemnly as would a Confederate jury handing down a death sentence. I quickly unclipped my own mask and fumbled it on before the dust had a chance to attack my unprotected eyes and lungs.

When we reached the bottom quarter of the cliff the car began a deceleration that almost brought me to my knees. I stepped shakily out onto the docks and took a deep breath. At sea level the air was thicker and richer.

Aboard the *Lunglance,* shipwrights were repaving the deck, gluing long translucent strips of whalebone plastic onto the deck with a thin watery adhesive. Already new masts had been stepped and a half-dozen ship's repairmen were replacing the lines aloft with tough new braided cables. I whistled softly to myself inside my mask. It had taken a substantial sum to get this much work done this quickly. Most whaling captains caught in a similar situation would have applied to the Arnar branch of their whaling corporations, but Desperandum had no such backing. All the money was his alone. Impressive.

Dalusa's tent was not set on deck. Not surprising. Shipwrights were repaving the spot where it was usually pitched. Perhaps Dalusa was aloft somewhere. I decided to ask Desperandum if he knew where she was. Although my obsession—already I was wondering if I should call it love—did not have Desperandum's wholehearted approval, I felt reasonably confident that he would tell me.

The hatch to Desperandum's cabin was open, so I went down the stairway into the dining room. Desperandum had been eating on board; the litter of several meals, dirty plates with congealing gravy, covered the captain's table.

I took off my mask and knocked on the door to Desperandum's cabin. "Come in," Desperandum rumbled.

I swung the door open and was instantly aware of a strained silence. Desperandum was seated in his swivel chair; by the bunk, standing stiffly and facing the captain, was the Nullaquan sailor, Murphig.

"Ah, Newhouse," Desperandum said with false joviality.

"Am I intruding?" I asked.

"No, no. Crewman Murphig here has just made me a rather interesting proposal. Would you like to tell him about it, Murphig?"

Murphig only stared sullenly at the wall.

"No? Well, Murphig learned that I am something of a scientist, and he came here to discuss . . . an apprenticeship."

I said nothing.

"But I'm afraid that Crewman Murphig and I differ rather radically on our ideas of the scientific method. Crewman Murphig has pronounced opinions."

Murphig had apparently reached the limits of his self-restraint. "You think we're barbarians, don't you?" he said tightly. "You come out of nowhere in those shiny interstellar ships, and you think you're dealing with a race of sub-humans. Well, God knows we're sinners. God knows we've lost some of our ideals, but that doesn't give you a right to treat us and our ideas like dirt."

Desperandum smiled indulgently. "Crewman Murphig is upset because I revealed to him that his ideas are more mystical than scientific."

"We're not blind," Murphig stated flatly. "We're not stupid. We don't talk about it, but we know there's something under the dust, something old and awful and strong. It . . . they . . . have been down there for millions of years, miles of dust over their heads, learning, living, always growing stronger, until they are wise in ways we can't possibly understand, until they're like . . . like gods of the deep."

"Gods of the deep," said Desperandum analytically. "A classic form of superstition. Understand, Murphig, that my refusal of your offer does not mean any lack of esteem for you personally. You're a fine sailor. But that's all you are."

"What about the sharks?" Murphig said. His mouth tightened. "I've been watching them. I've been watching *everything.*" He speared me with a quick glance. "They're always here when we kill a whale. They can't see it. They can't smell the blood, because the dust soaks it up. Their ears are tiny, they can't hear it. But they know when something has died. I watched you cut one up, Captain. I know their brains are very small. But they're cunning and vicious; they have more intelligence than any beast has a right to have."

"We've been over this before," Desperandum said resignedly. "They have pilot fish, remember? Surely you were watching them, little beasts with wings and large, perfectly functional eyes."

Murphig was silent.

"Have you had your say, crewman?"

"One more thing, Captain," said Murphig, his voice trembling with suppressed emotion. "We'll see by the end of the voyage whose ideas are closest to God's own truth. But I'll say this. You're putting your life and maybe more than your life in danger when you tamper with things you don't understand."

Abruptly, Desperandum burst into deep bass laughter. Finally, he stopped and wiped tears of laughter from his small, wrinkle-crusted eyes. "I apologize, Murphig, if I failed to show the proper regard for your people. It was just that until now I had never realized your potential for amusement."

Murphig's pale face turned paler. With clumsy, knotted hands, he pulled on his target-spotted dustmask, went through the cabin door, and then ran up the stairs three at a time.

"I didn't enjoy having to snub him like that," Desperandum said earnestly. "I like the man's attitude. But it's the gene pool, you understand. When a planet is settled exclusively by mystics, by religious fanatics, the fuzziest among us, those with the fewest redeeming tinges of rationality . . . well, I'm sure you understand, Newhouse."

"Yes, sir, I do."

"And when that situation is complicated by an essentially rigid and conservative culture . . . well, it's a question of human materials. You can't make an oscilloscope out of wood."

"Very true," I agreed.

Desperandum leaned back in his swivel chair; it adjusted with a creak. "What can I do for you, Newhouse?"

"I was wondering if you had seen—"

"Oh yes, the lookout woman. I seem to recall that our last conversation on this subject was broken off rather abruptly."

I said nothing, but tried to look a little chagrined. "Do you know where she is, sir?"

"I have a lot of respect for you, Newhouse, as a man, as a Terran, and of course as a cook. It's the first time I've eaten decently since I came to the crater."

"Thank you, sir."

"And I have a high regard for Dalusa, too. She was with me on both my previous voyages. But I view your relationship with considerable apprehension. I wonder if you've ever thought about the kind of motivation that would make a person change her planet, her body, even her entire species."

"She mentioned something about never quite fitting in."

"She was a freak," Desperandum said bluntly. "She was hideous. None of her, ah, tribe would touch her or talk to her. She was a pariah.

"Then the expedition came, creatures like gods in infection-proof suits. They were willing to talk. They were willing to tell their ideas to anyone who would listen. So, an occupational hazard, they were ripped to shreds." Desperandum shrugged. "So, Dalusa's tormentors died in hideous agonies, contaminated by the blood of their victims. When the next expedition came, as they always do, Dalusa was ready. And she left with them to go under the knives."

"A laudable decision," I said.

Desperandum frowned. "It's unwise to apply human standards to an alien, I know. But did it ever strike you that Dalusa might not be sane?"

"Captain, there are no objective standards for determining sanity. As you say, it is absurd to apply human standards to her, and, if she were insane by her own standards, I fail to see how it would be of any relevance to me. After all, I have no idea what poses for sanity among her native people, but from what you have told me, they seem markedly unpleasant."

"What if I told you it had something to do with blood?" Desperandum said. "Human blood, the agency of her salvation. What if I told you blood was her obsession, even a sexual fetish?"

"Frankly, Captain, I think I'd ask where you got your information."

There was silence for a few seconds. "I guess I won't tell you that then," Desperandum said finally.

"Then to turn to our earlier topic of conversation: I want you to keep a sharp eye on young Murphig. He won't jump ship. For a Nullaquan whaler, that's unthinkable. But he has been acting strangely lately. Sometimes sluggish, sometimes almost jittery, as if he were under the influence of some—" I held my breath while Desperandum searched for a word. "—some form of religious excitement. You have to expect a kind of prophet syndrome in cultures like this. If there's any unrest aboard the *Lunglance*, Murphig is likely to be at the center of it."

"I'll watch him, Captain," I promised.

"Fine. Oh, by the way. Could you clean up that mess on the dining table on your way out?"

"Captain," I said gently. "What about my question?"

It was then that I knew for sure that Desperandum was

88

an old man. A blank, almost terrified look flashed across his face, an expression I had seen before on the faces of old Timon Hadji-Ali and the Undines. A desperate search among the accumulated centuries of memory, memories packed and distorted by the inadequate human brain.

But Desperandum found it fast. "Dalusa. She's in the kitchen, waiting. Waiting for you."

I stacked the greasy dishes and put my mask back on. Then I carried them up on the deck, where the workmen were still working industriously, and went into the kitchen.

It was dark. I turned on the light switch with my elbow and set the dishes on the counter.

Dalusa was sitting on the stool next to the door leading into the ship's stores. She still had her mask on; her hands were folded at her throat and her wings hung from her arms like black velvet draperies.

I hoisted myself up on the counter next to the dishes and faced the woman. I took off my mask. "I want to talk to you, Dalusa. Won't you take off your mask?"

Dalusa reached for the strap on the back of her mask and slipped it up over her head slowly. Her attempt at drama was so transparent that I became impatient. But I restrained myself.

She lifted the mask slowly from her face, still keeping it between us so that I could not see her face. Then she suddenly dropped it.

I could feel the blood drain away from my face, could swear that I felt it trickling through a million arteries down into my neck and away. Dalusa's pale, ruined face turned gray in my vision. Feeling cold and sick, I gripped the edge of the counter with both hands.

Dalusa looked as if she had sucked on a spongeful of acid. Her mouth was swollen and hideous; her lips were so puffed and distorted that they looked like small purple sausages. White shreds of damp, dead skin adhered to the outer edges of her lips, and her ruined mouth was dotted with black and yellow ulcerated blisters.

I looked away. Then Dalusa spoke. I was so amazed that she was able to talk, that I almost missed her words. She talked slowly and lispingly, and her lips seemed to have an unnatural adherance. They parted stickily with every consonant.

"Do you see what you've done to me?"

"Yes," I said. It would only increase her torment to point out that it was more her responsibility than mine.

But she said nothing, and the silence stretched out agonizingly. Finally I said, "I had no idea that it would be so bad. The punishment is all out of proportion to the poor shred of Joy—God is cruel to you, Dalusa."

Her mouth moved painfully then, but I could not hear any words. "What?" I asked.

"Do you love me?" she repeated. "If you do, then it's all right."

"Yes, I do," I said, and though it had begun as a lie, when I finished I realized with a strange trapped bewilderment that I had told the truth.

Dalusa began to weep silently, thin glistening tears that slid down her pale perfect cheeks with unnatural speed to touch the swollen edges of her mouth. Almost reflexively, I stood up to embrace her, but stopped. Not for the first time, and certainly not for the last, I was torn by an aching frustration.

"You don't believe me," I said, and my mind made a sudden intuitive leap. "You want me to hurt like you do. Your love is pain, so you can't believe me unless I share your agony."

Dalusa moaned, a strange gutteral sound that made my hair stand on end. "Why, why can't we just touch each other? What have I done; what has been done to me?"

"Did you know I have a pair of gloves?" I asked.

Dalusa stared then broke into hysterical laughter. "Gloves? What are gloves doing on a whaling ship?" She suddenly leapt off the stool with a rustle of wings and, grabbing her mask, she ran clumsily up the stairs and out through the hatch.

I sat down on the stool and then sniffed at the air. Dalusa was wearing perfume.

Chapter 8
The Voyage Continues

After I finished the dishes I went back on deck. Dalusa had flown away. On my way back to the elevator I was met by a delivery boy from Merkle's Bar and Grill with my order of ale. He was wearing a plain black duskmast that marked him instantly as a lubber. I paid him and took the bottles down into the kitchen. Then I cleaned out the distilling equipment with a stiff wire bottle-brush and started brewing whiskey.

Growing hungry again, I decanted the loathsome stuff into a bottle and put it away in a cupboard. With luck, I would never have to drink it. Then I went back to the elevator. It crawled slowly up the shadowed side of the cliff. The sun was bisected by the western horizon, and the eastern wall of the crater was providing most of the light. The first stars were dim flecks on the darkening sky.

I went back to Starcross Street. There were no electrical display signs—they were forbidden by law—but heavy use had been made of the internal juices of Nullaqua's luckless bioluminescent life-forms. To my right, six unsteady Nullaquan whalers were forming a human pyramid, preparing to climb into the second-story window of a house of ill repute. Loud tuba music emerged from several of the bars, punctuated by the flatulent shrieks of Nullaquan cornets. I stepped over a mumbling merchant sailor and looked for a quiet restaurant. There weren't many, but I finally located one, an establishment that catered to Nullaqua's decrepit senior citizens. Like all cultures with heavy restriction of technology, Nullaqua simply did not have the rejuvenation techniques necessary to prolong life beyond even a single century. The life expectancy on Nullaqua was only ninety, and the doddering gaffers around me, their nose hairs white with age, looked every year of that.

Still, though the citizens dropped like mayflies, Nullaqua's civilization had remained fairly stable for the past four hundred years. And although the older generations were hurriedly shuffled into the crematoria, almost everyone was able to have a direct lineal descendant of some kind. The subtle but insidious psychological effects of adult life without children were still being measured by extra-Nullaquan social scientists. And on those advanced planets which did not restrict population growth, the life expectancy, not counting abortions, was only twenty-three. They killed a lot of children on planets like that. And of course, future shock and death-wish encroachment eventually got everyone, especially on advanced planets. Deep down, deep down, we all wanted to die.

But I was in no hurry, I reflected, digging into a tasty octopus pie with an aluminum fork. My appetite was only slightly diminished by stares of dotty curiosity from the resident Nullaquans. An off-worlder was still an unusual sight to some of these relics. I wondered if I should get a nose-wig. On the other hand, my eyelids would still betray my origin; they were not corrugated and my lashes were not dense enough to pass for native.

After supper I lost a little money in a casino, not enough to hurt, but enough to keep me entertained. Then I found a hotel, refused the daisy that the management offered, and tried to sleep. My slumber was fitful, as a chorus of intoxicated sailors reeled beneath my window once every half hour, singing obscene whaling songs. It was impossible to tell whether it was the same chorus each time; at any rate, the singing was uniformly bad. At last, annoyed, I took a blast of Calothrick's Flare, so potent that my ears rang like church bells and I left consciousness behind in a cloud of blue flame.

Next morning I was awakened by the shouts of a large crowd on Starcross Street, two blocks away. The *Lunglance* had had the bad luck to land on the eve of a local festival, one of the most important of the year: Growth Day. Festivities began with a wrestling contest. Wrestling bored me, so, after a leisurely breakfast in the hotel's restaurant, I went out and got drunk. Staggering into the street, I was accosted by a blonde Nullaquan daisy, who explained to me that she was offering special holiday rates. With unusual psychological insight for a Nullaquan, she even offered to clip her nose before our liaison.

There was no rational reason for refusal. She was cheap, clean, healthy, and devoid of any crippling emotional side effects. Also, I had been two months at sea.

But I was only beginning to plumb the depths of masochism that Dalusa had revealed to me. I gave the daisy a Nullaquan three-monune piece and told her to leave me alone.

But I had reckoned without the Nullaquan's hearty distaste for charity. She refused to take the money without performing a service in return. Obviously new to the trade, I thought tiredly. So, through a convolution of drunken logic that now seems incomprehensible, I told her to seek out Crewman Murphig of the *Lunglance* and convey to him apologies from John Newhouse. In return she could keep the money.

"Apologies for what?" she asked.

"If you're not gone by the time I count three I'll inform the Trade Synod," I threatened. She left in a hurry.

By now a parade was going on in the street. Parades have never held much appeal for me either, but, fortifying myself with a quarter-dropperful of Flare, I stood on the corner and watched the colors go by. I had trouble focusing my eyes. I seem to recall that a dozen Nullaquans came by directly in front of me, dressed in a gigantic black whale costume, but that may have been only a fiction of my fevered brain. Once in the mood, I kept feeding myself minimal doses of Flare, in order to maintain a steady glow.

Growing hungry, I bought a fried cylinder of meat-on-a-stick from a sidewalk vendor. I ate it to the accompaniment of a large and thoroughly incompetent brass band.

The *Lunglance* would set sail tomorrow morning. It was imperative that I be aboard before midnight. There was plenty of time left, though. My head was beginning to clear again and I took another short blast of Flare. A large battalion of Nullaquan urchins, clad in identical lilac blue uniforms, were marching down Starcross Street and chanting in unison. The sight would have been absolutely intolerable had I been sober.

I repressed any thoughts about Dalusa. Soon enough I would be back in the emotional pressure cooker of the *Lunglance*. At the thought a drug-inspired depression settled over me. Already I was beginning to feel sick, trapped, frustrated, and weak. A quick watery glimpse of Dalusa's blistered face appeared in my mind, and I shuddered. I was like a man sick almost to death with nausea, wanting to thrash and struggle but knowing it could only increase the misery.

The Flare was getting me down, I concluded suddenly. An enterprising Nullaquan had set up a bar outside his establishment and I ordered a light beer. I liked Nullaquan light beers, the lighter the better. The lightest ones were almost tasteless.

Four or five beers later I found myself on a whirring electric-powered commuter train, heading north to the second, northern, cluster of docks. From there one could take ferries to the other four islands in the Pentacle group. The train moved with irritating sluggishness, perhaps six miles an hour, the speed of a fast walk. I felt like getting out and pushing, but settled back against the whalehide seat, jostling the kerchief-headed, suspicious Nullaquan matron beside me. Her natural distrust of sailors was only amplified by my being an off-worlder.

The train cars were little metal and plastic cubicles with room for only four people. Each car had two whalehide couches, one facing forward, one backward. With the return of sobriety I noted that the two dour Nullaquan businessmen in the seats facing me were giving me the stern benefit of their attention. I looked away and leaned against the side of the car, letting one arm droop languidly over the side. The car had a sunroof, but no windows. It didn't need them. It never rained on Nullaqua.

Nullaquan sunsets were impressive, I noted comfortably

94

to myself sometime later. The train was returning from the docks and was full of mustachioed fishermen. Shrimpers, mostly. They waxed the ends of their mustaches.

The sun had already sunk in the west. Now the ridged edge of sunlight was slowly crawling up the eastern cliff wall. The light was much sharper, much less roseate than the dust-altered clifflight at sea level. Up and up it went, unnaturally sharp, already far above the limits of the atmosphere. The rocks had an albedo of around 30 percent, more in spots where long melted streaks had given the cliffside an obsidianoid sheen, piercingly bright where veins of metal were exposed. The stars were coming out.

The sunlight finished its performance by climbing to the lip of the cliffs. For an instant the broken crags at the very peak shone with stellar brilliance; then they winked out and joined the rest of the crater in shadowed dimness.

And at that very instant, calculated no doubt by parsimonious mathematicians, the Arnar streetlights came on. They were weak. The light in the railroad car flickered on also, a single dim yellow bulb set above our heads in the sunroof.

Only the areas around the cliffside elevators were well lit. There were no excuses for sailors. I piled into the elevator with a dozen glum Nullaquans, and we flew down the cliffside with stomach-turning speed.

The docks were lit, too. There was no chance of stumbling off a pier into the dust. And, there was a faint green glow by the docks. A sparse population of Nullaquan plankton had sprung up around them, nourished by water from occasional spills in loading and unloading.

The repairmen had finished their work; the *Lunglance* was in fine shape. The repair crew had even returned the tents and try-pots to the deck, now that it was newly sheathed in plastic. Government workers from the Synod of Ecology were loading whale eggs into the *Lunglance*'s port hull. The eggs, already fertilized, would be released overboard, three of them for every whale killed. It was no small task; the white, dimpled eggs were a foot across and weighed fifty pounds each. They came from the whale farm on another of the Pentacle Islands. There was a large depression in the top of one of the islands and it had been laboriously filled with dust, ton by ton. Now, captive whales fed and spawned in the shallow lake, and some attempts at specialized breeding were being made. Their young replenished the ocean, and for most of the incubation period their eggs were safe from the needle-beaked octopi that sucked most eggs dry and normally kept the whale population within bounds.

Very big on ecology, the Nullaquans. Very concerned with stability. Since I was growing a little dehydrated from processing the alcohol I had drunk, I went down to the kitchen for some water.

I had just finished my first glass when young Dumonty Calothrick came clattering down the stairs.

"Don't tell me," I said. "You were robbed. All your money's gone."

Calothrick looked puzzled. "Money? I got all my money. Somebody stole my Flare!"

"You mean that daisy didn't rob you blind?"

"Aw, death, no," Calothrick said impatiently. "She charged me a monune and a half for bed space and left me alone. I wasn't in the mood. Especially not with her." Calothrick shuddered. "Hey . . . you got some Flare left, right? Give me some."

I noticed for the first time that the whites of Calothrick's eyes were tinged with a film of yellow, a film like the thin striated layer that first forms on the surface of a pot of molten wax.

"I've got your packet," I said. "I took it when we were in the alley." I pulled the packet out of my shirt and held it out; Calothrick snatched it from my fingers. "You got the dropper too, huh?"

I handed him the dropper; he took it and glared at me resentfully. "You're sharp, Newhouse. Mighty sharp. I see you've been helping yourself." He looked at the lowered level of Flare in the packet and slurped up a full dropper.

"I was afraid you'd be searched. It's illegal now, remember?"

"Illegal. What makes you think any of these deadheads

would have known what it was? I would have told them it was medicine."

"You were pretty blasted."

"You must think I'm some kind of rube!" snapped Calothrick, tilting his head back and taking a blast from the eyedropper. "Get this straight. I may be young, but I'm not blind." He paused to belch. "You've been keeping most of the money and all of the Flare. I want some more. Maybe a bottleful. Especially if you're going to be using mine all the time."

I was angry. I stopped to yawn. "A bottle. What would you do with it? Where would you put it? The mates would find it for sure. If you want more, you can come down here after it."

Calothrick hesitated; the Flare was taking hold. "Well, listen, man," he said vaguely. "I'm not addicted to it or anything, see, but I'm getting more interested in it, and I feel like it'd be better if I always had some with me. What if it all gets stolen again? I need plenty. A couple of weeks' worth at least."

"How much is that?"

"Oh . . . about four dropperfuls a day . . . two or three packetfuls, I guess."

"You've got till midnight," I said. "Go up to Arnar and buy yourself some packets."

Calothrick left, scowling. Four droppers a day, I reflected. A dosage of that size would probably kill me. And if he kept it up at such a rate, Calothrick's brain cells would be destroyed. Burnt out. Unless he was of unusual physical resilience, Calothrick would be reduced to a condition of imbecility within a few years.

But it was his brain.

The *Lunglance* left at dawn, with a full company. After the two-day debauchery, the crew was more dour than ever. Not a word was exchanged at breakfast; the crew ate like sullen machines.

We sailed northeast. After two weeks we left the Pentacles behind. This part of the Sea of Dust was monopolized by a peculiar life form known as the lilypad. There were hundreds of acres of these strange plants. Their photosynthetic organ was a single round leaf, yards in diameter but less than an inch thick. It floated on the surface, spreading itself in order to absorb as much sunlight as possible. The gray sea was greenly polka-dotted with thousands of the plants; they were free floating and strangely sensitive. When disturbed, the leaf curled inwards, wrinkling over its entire surface and withdrawing completely into its root, a thick, round bulb. This immediately sank into the opaque depths, away from the reach of herbivores.

Many creatures lived in symbiosis or parasitism with the lilypad. Desperandum, who made a detailed study of the plant, isolated 257 separate species of associate organisms, including leaf nibblers, leaf miners, stem borers, leaf suckers, root feeders, and gall makers. Besides these there were twenty-six species of predators, fifty-five species of primary parasites, nine secondary parasites, and three tertiary parasites. Among all these creatures was a small six-legged crab that made a fine chowder. When our prows touched the lilypads they immediately shrank and sank, leaving their crabby passengers swimming frantically. Desperandum caught hundreds of the creatures simply by dragging a net after the ship.

Some of the lilypads were in bloom; they had a long straight stalk and a puffy white flower like a head of grain. Armored bees whined from stalk to stalk, scattering pollen. They were stingless, but inedible.

Everyone wanted chowder. Eventually I found a pair of crabcrackers in a bottom drawer, rattly geared objects with rusty hinges and sharp metal beaks, difficult to describe. One fitted a crab into a skeletal framework and pushed down on a worn plastic lever, neatly splitting its carapace and its legs.

The cook was expected to kill the crabs by dipping them in a dilute solution of his own blood. Nullaquans had a remarkably casual attitude toward bleeding. Besides, Dalusa, whose mouth had now healed so that only a few small black scabs were left on the edges of her lips, would be unable to help me as she had offered to do, if the crabs were contaminated with human blood. So I found a use for the whiskey after all. The alcohol seemed to act like a nerve poison on the crabs, producing a brief epileptic flurry followed by rapid death.

I cracked the poisoned crabs while Dalusa extraced their meat with her long, sharp-nailed fingers.

I still had my gloves. Our attempts to use them had resulted in failure. As soon as my gloved hands began to slide over her body, she burst into tears and hid her face in her wings. Perhaps, I thought, it was her inability to reciprocate that bothered her. She was unable to use the gloves once I had, because my palms were sweaty, understandably, and the insides of the gloves would have given her a rash. Logically, I boiled one of the gloves to remove contaminants, not realizing that its slick unstable plastics were vulnerable to heat. It melted.

But I still had one glove left. I have always had a vivid imagination and I was able to think of no less than five ways of using the glove to obtain mutual satisfaction. But Dalusa would have none of it. At the very sight of the glove she burst into tears and left the kitchen. It was disappointing, to say the least. I was able to see that there was a possible sordidness about the situation, but desperate times call for desperate action.

As a sort of compensation, Dalusa spent more and more time with me in the kitchen, making obviously false attempts at cheerfulness. She tried in her clumsy, artistically mutilated way to help with the cooking. I was touched by her attempt, so touched that I did not throw her out of the kitchen, although I could have done the work myself twice as quickly.

So we cracked crabs together.

After we had cleared the lily fields, Desperandum decided to do a sounding. He had come well prepared; he brought out another mile or so of superceramic fishing line and an immense lump of lead with a metal loop on top. Tying the line securely he heaved the lump overboard and then began to pay out line on a small winch.

In the shadow of the mainmast, Murphig was watching. He saw me watching him watch Desperandum, so he watched me for a while. It was an uncomfortable situation.

Desperandum got a depth of seventy-five feet. With a

smile he set the figures down in a small black logbook. Then doubt crossed his bearded features. He walked to the other side of the ship and paid out the line again. He got a depth of almost half a mile.

Apparently we were floating above the edge of a very steep plateau. Another would have shrugged and gone on. But Desperandum had the skepticism of the true scientist. He did the first sounding again and got a depth of a little less than six thousand feet.

The second sounding repeated got eight hundred feet.

Desperandum frowned belligerently and did the first sounding once more. He paid out all the line he had, two and a half miles, and still did not reach bottom. He hauled all the line back in, a process that took a full hour. He sat and thought for a while, then decided to do the second sounding again.

He reached a depth of nine thousand feet and then the line went limp. Desperandum reeled it back in. Something seven thousand feet down had neatly sliced the line.

Desperandum's face did not change at the sight of the sliced line, but hard knots of muscle appeared on the sides of his jaws, making his dustmask bulge.

I went back down to the kitchen. Dalusa was out on patrol. Soon I would have to start work on the third meal of the day, traditionally eaten by clifflight.

I always planned my menus a week in advance. I was looking up my reference for the night when the hatch creaked open and in came Murphig.

I looked up and tried to relax the muscles that had instantly tightened at the sight of him. I had never learned how much he knew about our syncophine operation, and I had been unable to think of a way of plumbing his knowledge without revealing yet more.

"What can I do for you?" I said.

"I've been meaning to come down and talk," Murphig said, pulling off his targeted dustmask. "I got the message you sent in Arnar. The one through the daisy."

I cast my mind back two weeks. I had indeed sent a message. I had assumed that my memory of the action was a

100

fever dream of some kind. I had apologized to Murphig, as I recalled.

"Yes," I said. "I was sorry to have broken in on your discussion with the captain."

"What did you think of it?" Murphig said, looking at me sharply.

"I thought he gave your ideas rather short shrift."

"Decent of you to notice that," Murphig said almost airily. His eyes were dark, like chips of brown glass, and his nostril hair, I noticed, had been clipped into neat globes rather than the traditional wiry bush. His accent was lighter than a Nullaquan's, too; it was almost galactic. It was obvious that he came from an upper-class family; perhaps his parents were bureaucrat/clergy.

"You saw the results of the sounding. What did you think?"

"Puzzling."

"It fits in well with my theories. I've been thinking about the crater lately. About the air. Suppose that at one time Nullaqua had an atmosphere. Then the sun flared and blew it away. But suppose that an intelligent race had already evolved, a race that could see it coming. They would dig a shelter, a vast shelter with room enough for a whole civilization. A giant shelter with seventy-mile-high walls and a layer of dust to insulate them from the radiation. Then, after the catastrophe, the traces of air would leak back in. Eventually the Old People would get used to the dust down there; they would be unable to live without it, perhaps even change their physiques to live without air. . . .

"Once they were very strong; you can tell because of those Elder Culture outposts at the top of the cliffs. They didn't dare come into the crater. They might have been . . . eaten? So now they are much weaker. All they want is peace, stasis, mutual ignorance. They don't want to hurt or kill, but those that disturb their perfection will be obliterated, silently, swiftly. Already men have lived here five centuries, and though there are rumors, folktales, unconfirmed sightings, mysteries of the deep, there's nothing really solid. So they may be dying. Or maybe they're only asleep. But they are there, that's certain."

Murphig's face had flushed slightly with excitement while he spoke; now he sat on the stool with a sigh.

"Murphig," I said slowly, "that's the most ridiculous thing I ever heard."

The sailor flushed with anger, abruptly pulled on his mask, and left the kitchen.

Chapter 9

A Further Conversation with the Lookout

After supper, an excellent crab chowder, Desperandum sent his cabin boy, Meggle, to call me to his cabin. I went, and found Desperandum in his swivel chair. The desk before him was covered with scattered papers. Overhead was a single whale-oil lantern; it cast odd shadows on Desperandum's broad, bearded face.

Desperandum leaned back in his chair and laced his fingers behind his head. "You've been showing some interest in science lately, Newhouse," he said without preamble, "so I thought I'd explain to you exactly what I was doing today and what I proved."

"That's very thoughtful of you, Captain."

"Let's take the evidence and examine it dispassionately, shall we?" said Desperandum in a tone so elaborately dispassionate that I was overcome with distrust. "The line stopped at variable heights, then was sliced on the way down. What does that suggest to you?"

"Playfulness," I said.

Desperandum glared. "I made some calculations," he said, ignoring my remark. He indicated the papers on his desk. I looked at them.

"Calculations based on the properties of granulated rock. You see, I took the specific gravity of the rock, and electrostatic and chemical bonding as a function of surface area. And I applied this data to well-known geological formulae for the formation of metamorphic rock."

I continued to look at the papers on the desk. It was a

little difficult to make out the figures on the paper, but I was doing it.

"It turns out that the dynamics of the Sea of Dust are more complex than we had suspected," Desperandum continued blithely. "Under certain conditions, which cannot be duplicted here on the surface, the dust is fused by pressure into long thin horizontal strata of flattened rock. They are always shifting and being eaten away; they are highly unstable. But they're stable enough to stop a plumb line, and the edges are thin and sharp, like flint. They can cut."

"So that was what did it," I said. I had just realized that the papers I had been studying were indeed covered with numbers. But there was no sign of any computation. There were three or four scattered multiplication signs, and a pair of large integrals, but they had nothing to do with the numbers themselves. There were no totals. Only numbers. Large numbers, too, numbers in the millions and billions, as if adding comma after comma gave the numbers an increased significance, a stronger hold on reality. The other papers were the same. Meaningless random scribblings.

"Yes, that's it," Desperandum said kindly. "There's other confirmation, too. One can see that barriers like that would give rise to freakishly strong currents. Imagine, for instance, if a rock barrier separating two thermoclines suddenly gave way. There would be a sudden turbulence. Perhaps giving rise to a storm."

"Very convincing," I said. Our eyes met in a quick mutual flash of suspicion.

Later that night, much later, I was awakened by a whispered tread on the stairs. Only one person could walk so lightly, Dalusa.

It was almost totally dark, so dark that strange dim purples and maroons moved nebulously across my field of vision. When I looked up through the hatch from my pallet on the kitchen floor, I could see a single weak dust-filtered star.

It was cold at night on the Sea of Dust. The dust did not have the heat-holding, weather-tempering properties of water. I slept in my pallet, a stitched quilt of black and white hexagons pulled up to my chin.

"Dalusa," I said. My voice sounded unnaturally loud in the silence.

"I wanted to talk," she whispered. I heard her walk toward me. Were her eyes better in the dark than mine? Perhaps she could see the infrared waves I radiated, or could see by the light of the single star. At any rate, she came unerringly closer, adjusted the edge of the quilt around my chin, and rested her cheek on my chest. The quilt separated us, but I could feel the heat of her body and the weight. She weighed no more than a child.

My pulse accelerated; I sought calmness. "What did you think of our captain's antics today?"

"It was nothing new," she murmured, snuggling closer. She put her hands on my biceps, under the quilt. I felt a sudden niggling urge for a blast of Flare. I tried to forget it.

"What do you mean?"

"I've been on three trips with the captain," she said. "In all that time I think I've seen him do twenty soundings, perhaps, and he never succeeds. Sometimes he accepts the first figure. Sometimes he keeps trying. There are never two that are the same."

"You mean he's done it all before?"

"Time and time again. With a new crew each time, except for me."

I laughed in the dark. Dalusa stirred against me. The whole situation was so tragically ludicrous that the only human responses were to laugh or get drunk. It was too late at night to drink. "Why does he do that? Why does he keep fighting it?"

Dalusa moved and I could sense, but not see, her face looming only inches above mine. Her hot breath, faintly redolent of alien spices, touched my nose and mouth. "Did you ever think that Captain Desperandum might not be sane?"

A powerful surge of déjà vu overcame me. "Don't tell me that it's an obsession," I muttered.

"But it is," Dalusa said sweetly. "You know that in very old people, the urge to die begins to grow more and more powerful. Death comes in ways that no one understands.

But you can live, I think they say, if you have a purpose, a goal, something that means so much to you that every cell in your body knows about it and stays alive for its sake."

I tried absentmindedly to embrace her, keeping the blanket between us. But I had forgotten that her wings were attached to the sides of her torso, all the way down to the short ribs. I settled for putting my hands over her buttocks.

Dalusa continued unheedingly, "That's what Desperandum wants to do. He wants to live, on and on and on. But the mind is tricky. When you war against yourself you can only lose."

"I have every confidence in the captain," I said. I was sure that he would find a way to kill himself.

I lifted my knees, slowly, and Dalusa settled luxuriously against my groin. She rested her sharp chin on my chest. "I love you," she said.

"I love you too." It was still true.

We were silent for a few seconds. "I can hear your blood moving," Dalusa whispered.

There followed several minutes of extreme frustration. Afterwards, I felt I had reached the apex of a new emotion, one previously unknown to me, a grotesque hybrid of lust and anger that found its culmination in pain. Dalusa's sudden whimpered gasp as I caught her elbow in a viselike grasp was music to my ears.

At last the realization of my sadism hit me and I released her arm.

Dalusa drew in a loud ragged breath, close to my ear.

I gritted my teeth. "There was no satisfaction in it, no climax—"

My complaint was cut off suddenly when Dalusa punched me in the stomach. Her clenched fist was backed by all the massive strength of her shoulders and pectorals; it hit so hard that a vivid red flash showed before my eyes and air gusted from my lungs.

"Better now?" Dalusa asked melodiously.

I clenched my fist to break her teeth in, but realized suddenly that it *was* better. It was my first insight into the joy of pain.

"You hurt me," I said.

"I'm sorry," she said contritely. "You started it; I thought that was what you wanted. Please don't be angry." She stiffened miserably against me.

"I'm not like you," I said after a long silence. "You can't expect me to hurt like you do. I can't bleed for you, Dalusa. I can't, and I won't. If you can't face that, maybe we should forget the whole thing."

"We'll see how things will be," she whispered, and her thick dull hair fell gently over my face.

Chapter 10
Flying Fish

My next days were occupied mostly by cooking. I spent much time studying Nullaquan tastes, thinking that when I returned to Reverie I would startle my friends with odd Nullaqua-style delicacies. Unfortunately, while she was sweeping the kitchen Dalusa accidentally upset the container of horseradishlike spice into one of my stews. A single taste of this inadvertent dish puckered my mouth for two hours. I almost threw it out, but served it at the last minute. The crew ate it with their usual stolidity and attention. Had Nullaqua grown trees, they would have eaten the bark and found it good.

There was not much wind in this part of the Sea of Dust. The equator was at the verge of the two convection cells that determine the crater's climate, and eternal calm stretched from wall to wall. The air was clearer, too, and to either side of *Lunglance* a silvery heat haze stretched shimmering into the distance. One could squint through the lenses of one's mask and almost imagine the *Lunglance* serenely afloat on a monstrous ocean of mercury. The sky seemed bluer than usual here, almost violet, and the low rim of cliffs, far to the west, were tinged purple with distance. Every scrap of plastic sail that the *Lunglance* had was set, even the tiny auxiliary ones at the very top whose masts were no thicker than broomsticks. Only the merest whisper of wind propelled us and the ship seemed to slide almost regretfully through the dust.

I was sweating inside my mask; I had to tilt my head back and shake it to keep perspiration out of my eyes. The crew, with thicker eyebrows than mine, had no such problem. I leaned over the rail again and stared moodily into the distance, still a little glazed from the Flare I had done that morning. It was an affecting scene, I noted. I thought about writing a poem. I decided against it.

Dalusa, back from her morning patrol, swooped by me at the rail, so close that the wake of her passage stirred my hair. I waved in acknowledgement. Dalusa, I noticed, was getting her own equivalent of a tan; she was growing paler and paler with repeated exposure to the sun. It was a more logical arrangement than my own. After all, pale skin reflects the heat.

I looked around unobtrusively and was relieved to find Murphig nowhere in sight. I had been sure that he was standing around somewhere, watching.

Perhaps I would have to make a friend of Murphig. He was an open, inquiring mind, and despite his oddities he seemed firmly rooted in sanity. Suppose, for instance, that Desperandum suddenly became dangerous. Little help could be expected from the tradition-bound mates or oxlike crew. They would probably poison their mothers before they would soil their souls with mutiny. Calothrick was a zero, also. He was still resentful because I had not given him his own store of Flare, as I had learned just yesterday when he had come back to fill up all three of his packets. He was growing dirtier, too; his hair was lank and greasy, and the lightning-stripes were slowly peeling off the sides of his mask. He could not be trusted.

And it would take at least two of us to handle Desperandum; it would probably take two just to kill him, even with the harpoons. I even had my doubts about Dalusa as a confederate. She loved me, there was no doubt about that. But in what way? How much did love mean to her, anyway? There was no way to tell, as she refused to talk about her cultural background. Dalusa obsessed me but I was not yet blind.

We killed two whales later that day and dropped six fertilized eggs overboard. I cooked whale steaks that night. They were noxious.

Next morning there was a cloud on the southern horizon. This could only bode ill, as Nullaqua never had the decent, normal clouds of harmless vapor that grace the skies of other planets.

"What do you make of it, Mr. Flack?" I heard Desperandum say to his first mate, handing the man a pair of binoculars.

"Flying fish, sir," replied the laconic whaler.

"Good! Good!" said Desperandum gruffly. "Mr. Flack, have two men ready to help me with equipment. The rest of the crew will retire belowdecks."

While two crewmen dragged monitoring devices from Desperandum's cabin, the rest of us sought shelter below. Before I went in, I glanced quickly around for Dalusa. She was nowhere in sight. I later discovered that she had gone below before I did. I sat on the stool in the kitchen while the rest of the crew tramped down the stairs. Calothrick walked by and gave me a glazed, yellow-toothed grin.

I debated a short blast of Flare while the migration passed. The pro side was winning when Flack stuck his head through the hatch and said flatly, "Cookie wanted on deck."

I went. On deck, Desperandum and the two crewmen were stringing nets between the masts. I noticed that six cubical boxes with swiveling wire-mesh radar dishes had been set several feet apart in front of the nets. Red and blue wiring trailed in tangles from the boxes to a sort of metal pillbox, fitted together out of five thin sheets of iron. It had a thick visorlike window, facing south toward the cloud. Already the sails had been furled, to give the migratory horde leeway. In the feeble winds of the equator, we could not possibly have outrun or dodged the fish.

The nets were ready. "Get below, men," Desperandum told the crewmen. They hastened into the hold and slammed the hatch behind them. Already the fish swarm was assuming ominous proportions.

"Newhouse!" the captain shouted. I walked closer and saluted. "This way if you please," Desperandum continued. He opened a low door in the side of the metal pillbox and we walked inside. Touching switches, Desperandum turned on a dim light in the ceiling and set an air filter humming.

They were rather cramped quarters, only seven feet by seven feet, and Desperandum's vast bulk took up much of that. In addition, there was a metal counter that supported Desperandum's binoculars and a large flat tally box with a small television screen. Two tiny white blips crossed the screen, starting from the top and moving slowly and erratically.

Desperandum reached under the counter and handed me a notebook and a pen. "You can take off your mask," he said. "The filters should have cleaned the air by now."

I took off my mask and dropped it under the counter. "You can write, I hope," Desperandum said.

"Certainly, Captain," I said.

"Good. You're here to take notes. Copy down the numbers I give you into that column I've listed as 'individuals.' Understand?"

"Yes, sir," I said, taking the notebook and lodging it in the crook of my left elbow.

"Two," said Desperandum. "We'll be just on the fringes of the horde for a few minutes, so you can take it easy. Stay alert though. You want to look before they arrive?"

Without waiting for an answer he handed me the binoculars. I stooped to get them at the level of the visor, which was set at Desperandum's height. I focused the binoculars.

The cloud resolved itself into thousands of individual fish, foot-long creatures with thin, brightly colored wings. They dipped and pirouetted like the molecules of a gas.

"They look like butterflies," I said.

"What are butterflies?"

"Earth fauna. Six-legged invertebrates with multicolored wings. They sometimes travel in swarms."

"Are they aquatic?"

"No, sir."

"Well, the analogy might be worth pursuing anyway," Desperandum rumbled. "Eighty-seven."

I wrote the number down. A complex pattern of clumped and scattered dots appeared on Desperandum's television screen; he did a quick sketch of the pattern on graph paper in his notebook. "See how many we have in the nets," he said.

I crouched to look out.

"Uh . . . Captain . . ."

"What?"

"They're slicing the nets to pieces out there. Their wings are as sharp as razors."

Desperandum's ruddy face turned pale. He looked out the window and grunted, as if he had been struck in the stomach. He looked down with an attitude of intense concentration and touched two switches on his tally box.

"Three hundred and ninety-three," he said.

There was a light metallic thud as a flying fish struck our pillbox. Desperandum flinched. There were more thuds.

The main body of the swarm was passing over the *Lunglance*. "One four nine four three," Desperandum said, sketching frantically. The television screen was alive with swarming dots. "Aren't we catching any of them?" Desperandum demanded.

I looked out and flinched myself when a fish struck the window. "No, sir," I said. "The nets are completely shredded now, they're just lying on the deck. There're a few fish on the deck by the mizzenmast, though. Wait a minute. They just flew off."

"Five five six two seven," Desperandum said. The air was growing dark. There were millions of them out there. "No matter," said Desperandum, recovering his poise. "We've still got the radar to analyze their flying pattern. Their spawning grounds are in a bay just behind the Brokenfoot Islands. We can stop there and pick up a few specimens."

"That's a bit of a detour, Captain," I said. It was an unwise remark.

"I'll thank you to remember that I am the captain of this ship," Desperandum said.

"I apologize, sir. I was out of line."

It sounding like hail on the top of our pillbox; dozens of fish were colliding and rebounding. "Two oh five, eight eighty-three," Desperandum said.

Then, suddenly, part of Desperandum's television screen went dark, a long narrow vertical band on the left side of the screen. Desperandum frowned mightily and touched switches with his thick, blunt fingers. The band stayed dead.

"They must have sliced the wiring from one of my radar sets," Desperandum said. "That means I'll have to multiply the rest of the values by a sixth. Make a note of that. One eighty-five, nine forty-one."

I glanced at the screen. White dots were pouring off the live portions of the screen into the dead area. None were re-emerging.

"What are they doing out there?" Desperandum asked himself. He peered through the visor; three fish, their thin crystalline wings splashed with yellow and crimson, collided with it at once. Desperandum flinched back.

Another band of the screen went dead. "One oh one three two," Desperandum said. "Are they thinning out, or are they just flying into the dead areas?"

I bent and looked out. "It does seem to be getting a little clearer, Captain."

"Any in the nets?"

"No, sir. But there are several dozen by the radar installations. One of them isn't moving. Its wing seems to be shrivelled. It must have been electrocuted. Now a thick band of them is coming over the rail. They just hit a radar box and knocked it over."

I glanced down at Desperandum's screen. The radar was pointing straight upwards, and its values did not mesh with the others'. There was no longer a coherent image; dots were leaping madly in and out of existence along the zone between the areas on the screen that were covered by the fourth and fifth radar sets.

"We're going blind," Desperandum said.

"They seem to be attacking the boxes," I said. Another area of the screen winked out.

"Yes," Desperandum said. "They must operate by radar themselves. The signals probably confuse their own flying patterns. That's why they collide with the boxes. It would be interesting to see how they do it." Another section of the screen went dead. I looked out the window.

"Only the first, fourth, and fifth boxes are working, Captain," I said. "That's where all the fish are, too. The other boxes are deserted. Hmmm. I was mistaken about that electrocuted fish. Captain. It's still alive, and trying to fly off. It's having difficulties though."

"I must have one of those specimens," Desperandum said tightly, shutting off the screen with a snap. The fish rose and fluttered away. "Put your mask on, Newhouse. I'm going to open the door."

I grabbed my dustmask. "Don't do it, Captain. You'll be sliced to ribbons."

"Don't try to stop me," Desperandum bristled. "When I aim to find something out, I don't let anything stand in my way." He put his arm against my shoulder and brushed me casually out of the way. I slammed into the back of the pillbox and saw stars. Hurriedly I pulled on my dustmask, then reached out and slammed the door shut.

I heard a flutter. Somehow one of the damnable little beasts had flown inside the pillbox. I grabbed the notebook with both hands and looked around wildly. Something touched my sleeve near the elbow and I saw a red and yellow flash out the corner of my eye. I swung quickly, heard a solid *whop* and a thud as the fish struck the wall. It slid crippled and thrashing to the ground, leaking ichor from around one of its flat, lidless eyes. Its dotted wings were broken, but their razor edges still gleamed evilly in the light from the overhead bulb. It did look a lot like a butterfly. I had seen one in a book once.

I looked at my sleeve. There was a neat two-inch slash just above my elbow, but the skin was untouched.

I dropped the notebook on the crippled fish, pinning it down, and looked out to see how Desperandum was doing.

He had seized a whaling spade from somewhere and broken it, leaving a five-foot metal stub with a flat spade at one end, like a flyswatter. The fish were not attacking him. What few were left were evading him with insolent ease and fluttering languidly off to join their brothers in the departed swarm. Desperandum swung at them with all his massive strength, but they floated serenely up and around the edges of the spade.

Suddenly one dipped and swooped near him. It seemed

114

to miss him, but suddenly a bright red line appeared on the side of his neck. Desperandum bellowed and swiped at the thing with one hand, knocking it to the deck. Blood dripped from his fingers. The creature struggled to rise, but Desperandum leapt suddenly and mashed it to paste under the heels of his boot. Blood was trickling down the side of his neck and into his shirt. A quick feint with the spade and a stab downed another; he swatted it to the deck. It splattered. Then he ran after the retreating cluster of fish and halved one with the spade's metal edge. Its head flew overboard. Another fish swooped down from nowhere and scored his arm. With astonishing speed Desperandum snatched it in midair and squeezed it juicily, earning more cuts in the process. More splatters of blood marred the deck.

The few remaining fish were fluttering upward now, gaining height and moving out of the captain's reach. There was no point in attacking him. It would have taken hundreds of such shallow wounds to drain the gallons of blood in Desperandum's massive frame.

The entire flock was gone. I opened the pillbox door and glanced quickly at the receding horde. The last few fish were struggling to regain their positions in the flock.

Bleeding, Desperandum watched them recede into the distance. Then he threw his bloodied spade aside with a clatter and walked to the pillbox.

"We have a few specimens now," he said. "It's too bad, but I think their heads were all crushed. That would be where they kept their radar equipment. What a shame."

He walked inside the pillbox and disconnected a few of the wires from the tally box.

I pulled my mask off and closed my eyes. "One of the fish flew in here, Captain. I managed to trap it," I said all in a breath. I pulled my mask back on and inhaled. Dust stung my nose. I sneezed and nearly burst my eardrums. Desperandum shut the door with a loud clang and turned on the air filters. "Really? Where?"

I waited for the air to clear, then pulled off my mask and said, "I think it's still alive. Right under that notebook."

"Notebook? Where?" Desperandum looked at the

counter. He took a step back and—squish—his large flat foot landed squarely on the book. I winced.

"Well. What a misfortune," Desperandum said in a tone of deep regret. He picked up the notebook and gazed critically at the stickily adhering remnants of fish. "Completely ruined. What bad luck. By the way, Newhouse, I'm sorry I snapped at you a few minutes ago. I was overwrought."

"I understand, sir. I had it coming, anyway."

"No, no, I appreciate frankness. And, as you said, I don't think the crew would appreciate a detour like that. There aren't many whales there; they would see it as a waste of time. We don't want the men getting restless."

"Just as you say, sir."

"You're dismissed. Give the men the all clear when you go back to the kitchen. And have our medical officer report to my cabin."

"Yes, sir." I left.

And that was the last of the incident. But, later I found Dalusa staring raptly at the dried patches of Desperandum's blood on the deck. I scrubbed it clean with sand that night when no one was looking.

Chapter 11
The Cliffs

Desperandum healed fast, except for his arm. He painted the slash with iodine but refused to cover the ugly black webwork of stitches put in by our first mate.

We continued to sail northwards and soon passed the halfway mark of our voyage, the Brokenfoot Islands. The settlements here had the best hydroponics labs on Nalluqua. They grow 90 percent of Nullaqua's tobacco and over half the grain used in brewing beer. We did not land but exchanged greetings with several merchant vessels and a shrimp boat. I bought a new jackknife from an old man in a trading skiff.

I had lost my first knife to the glue in the false compartment of the *Lunglance*. I had often thought of confronting Desperandum directly with my knowledge of those hidden stores. It might even be possible that he did not know about the engine, the propeller, and the tanks of oxygen. But I decided against it.

We killed four more whales and laboriously butchered them. There were sharks here, too. They were a different subspecies from the sharks at the Seagull Peninsula, but they had the same vicious teeth, the same flying pilot fish, and the same disquieting hints of intelligence. Ignoring his wounds, Desperandum attacked the creatures with the rest of the crew, wielding a long whaling spade with extreme viciousness and every ounce of his incredible strength. The sharks attempted to give Desperandum a wide berth, and once a flying fish escaped Dalusa's nets and bit a small piece out of Desperandum's right ear, leaving it scalloped.

Desperandum snatched the fish from midair and stamped it to juice under his boot. After that he went after the eyes of the sharks. Blinded, they responded with suicidal ferocity, ramming the *Lunglance*'s sides with their snouts and leaping out of the dust to chew blindly on the railing. When the railing was down they chewed on whatever they could reach.

So far it had not been crewmen. Seeing the captain's excessive joy in slaughter, the crew grew nimble with apprehension. And the blinded sharks did not have long to strike. It never took Desperandum more than two seconds to spear his shark-slimed spade into the vital organs.

By now we were approaching another Landmark.

There had always been cliffs on the horizon, rugged battlements whose roseate clifflight shed a crescent lunar glow at twilight. But now we were approaching the steepest edge of the Nullaqua Crater, that fifty-mile-long geological phenomenon known simply as the Cliffs.

The Cliffs are seventy miles high. They beggar description. I believe I could write for hours without conveying the actual visceral impact of seeing something that is seventy miles high. But I'll try.

How quickly can a man climb? Two miles a day, perhaps? Two miles, then. Reader, you would be two miles above sea level before you were even over the *boulders* that have piled at the foot of the Cliffs. After two days of climbing you would find it impossible to breathe. Putting on an oxygen mask you could possibly climb another mile. Then you would have to switch to a spacesuit. The sky would turn black before you were halfway up the Cliffs. After a month you would be climbing rock not disturbed in four billion years. Up there it is old, it is cold, it is dead. There is no wind up there to disturb the slow eons of dust. There are no rivers to carve the rocks, no water to freeze and split open cracks, no bushes or lichen to seek out flaws in the cliffside with clever fingers and patient tenacity. Perhaps, once a decade, a soundless trickle of dust cascades down the ancient rock to the dessicated sea below.

Eventually, sometime, you would reach the lip of the cliff. You would stand in an airless badlands of tortured, buckled rock, that is the silent, day-long victim of dreadful heat and deadly cold.

Turn and look behind you, reader. Can you see the crater now? It is wide, round, magnificent; within it shimmers a sea of air above a sea of dust. Almost a million human beings live within this titanic hole, this incredible crater, this single staring eye in the face of an empty planet.

* * *

"In less than two months we ought to be docking safe and sound in the Highisle," I told Dalusa, hugging her through the blanket. She gave a little moan of appreciation, and I grinned in the dimness.

"You said you wanted to leave Nullaqua," I said.

"Yes."

"So do I. And I'll be coming into a sizable amount of money soon after we dock." In about four months, I calculated roughly. Long enough to inform the Flare dealers on Reverie of the tight conditions and my last big haul. A few samples of my brain-kicking brew and they would move heaven and earth to get me back. All hope was not lost. I knew chemists on Reverie. Perhaps they could synthesize Flare. Maybe even improve it.

"Plenty of money. Enough to pay our way off planet, both of us."

There was no reply.

"I know the situation looks hopeless for us," I said, emphasizing the *looks*. "But nothing's impossible with money. You can have your whole body chemistry altered; or, if that's too difficult, I'll alter mine. We can live together for years, maybe centuries. Even have children, if you want them."

Still nothing. I did not allow the silence to become uncomfortable.

"I feel that we have something here, a relationship, that could be very strong, very long lasting," I said. "I don't know why, but I do love you, I love you very much. So"— I reached under the blanket and pulled out a ring, one of the few that I had brought with me on my voyage. I think I

119

mentioned that I have a fondness for rings. This was one of my favorites, a small Terran amphibious quadruped wrought in silver, one of its long powerful legs stretched in a circlet and touching its chin. I wore it on my little finger.—"I brought you this ring. There is an ancient Terran custom I want to observe that involves it. It's called betrothal. If you wear it, it symbolizes our emotional dedication to one another and to no other persons."

"The ring is very beautiful," Dalusa said hoarsely. I looked up at her; tears glistened dimly on her face. I was touched, having always thought that "weeping for joy" was only an expression.

"Don't put it on yet," I said hastily. "I haven't sterilized it."

"And when I do put it on, then we will be formally betrayed?"

"Betrothed," I corrected.

Dalusa began to weep aloud. "I'm afraid," she said. "I'm afraid you'll hate me, want to cast me out. I think you'll look at me and wonder how you ever could have wanted me. What will I do when I lose you?"

"But you won't," I said. "I'll love you as long as this personality exists; I'm sure of that. God knows we'll change; we'll both change. But there are decades, centuries ahead of us both. When the time comes, you can decide what you want to do."

"I'm afraid—"

"I'll protect you. It's a promise." I stirred. "Come on, let's boil the ring. Then you can put it on."

Dalusa stood up and wiped her eyes with one hand. "Where will we go when the voyage is over?"

"To Reverie. You'll like it there. It still has wilderness; population control is strict; the climate is very agreeable. I lived there before I came to Nullaqua. I still have friends there."

"What if they don't approve of us?"

"Then they won't be my friends any more. I . . . we don't need them." I put a pot on the stove, poured a few ounces of water into it, and set it to boil. I dropped in the ring.

"Don't look so downhearted, Dalusa," I said. "Give me a smile. There's a good girl. Think of it. Maybe we can arrange an actual Terran marriage, a traditional one. I doubt if there are any Terran religious sects on Reverne, but we can probably find a monotheist of some sort who'd be willing to preside. And after the operations we can live together in a way that approaches normality . . . except of course that few men are privileged to have a wife so beautiful."

She smiled for the first time.

"Neither one of us can be strictly called normal," I said, checking the ring in the boiling water. "But that doesn't mean we have to be miserable. We have as great a right to a life without misery and suffering as anyone else. No more pain, no more blisters or blood—"

I fished the ring out of the boiling water with a pair of pincers and waved it in the air to cool.

"Maybe we should wait," Dalusa said finally, her dark eyes following the movements of the ring. "Maybe after we are on land again, when you have a chance to see normal women, maybe you won't love me any more." She seemed almost desperate.

My face didn't move but I frowned internally. "I know my own mind. I think the ring's cool now. Do you want it?"

She took it.

Chapter 12

Anemones

Once we were past the Cliffs, Desperandum threw his nets overboard again and tugged them sluggishly behind the ship. I wondered what he was after. Plankton was sparse here.

While he waited, Desperandum went below into the storeroom. He soon emerged with a folding table under one arm and a huge glass jar or urn in his other hand. It was one of the largest glass containers I had ever seen. I could have curled up inside of it. It was cylindrical, as wide as it was tall, and it had no lid.

Desperandum lumbered over by the mainmast and set the jar down with a clink. Then he opened the folding table with precise snaps, straightening its legs. From a large cloth pocket on the bottom of the table he pulled out four large suction cups, plastic ones as large as dinner plates. Rubbery knobs on the tops screwed neatly into the bottoms of the table legs. Desperandum fitted on the cups, turned the table right side up, and set it on the deck. He put a little of his massive weight on the table and the suction cups flattened instantly. It would have taken at least five men to tear that table loose.

I noticed that the tabletop had a wide circular indentation in it, just the size of the bottom of the glass jar. Sure enough, Desperandum picked up the jar and set it neatly into the hole. He stepped back to admire his work.

"Mr. Bogunheim!" Desperandum rumbled.

"Yes, sir?" said the third mate.

"Have this jar filled up with dust. About three-quarters of the way to the top will do."

Soon Calothrick and a scrawny Nullaquan deckhand were busy carrying buckets. Desperandum retired to his cabin.

There were odd convection currents in that tubful of dust. Particles heated by sunlght through the wall of the jar crept upwards along the side of the glass and diverged across the surface. Cooler dust flowed sluggishly to replace it. The patterns of circulation would change as the sun slid across the sky.

Day was evenly divided here at the center of the crater. Morning lasted five hours. There was no waiting for morning in the dry shadow of the eastern cliffs as we had in Arnar. In the Highisle dusk came early. It came at the same time every day, and the sun rose at the same spot. Nullaqua had an axial tilt of less than a degree. There were no seasons, no weather to speak of, only sameness, constancy, stasis both physical and cultural, forever and ever, amen.

After the last meal of the day Desperandum retrieved his net. He spread it gently on the deck. There were dozens of hard little nuggets in it: three or four hundred pebbles of green-faceted plankton, small white pearls of fish eggs, wormlike coiled cylinders, greenish-speckled ovoids, flattened spheres marked with broken brown lines against cream white. There was even a spiny, shiny black egg as large as my fist.

Desperandum kneeled and began to sort his catch, making quick notes in an open booklet. Then the selected eggs and some of the plankton went into the tub of dust. Desperandum sent a crewman down to the kitchen for water; when the man returned, Desperandum sprinkled a few ounces over the dust.

"They'll hatch soon," Desperandum told me. "Then we'll see what we've got."

I nodded; Desperandum left. It was getting colder now that the sun had set. The dust was flowing in a different way; it cooled at the surface and slid away down the sides of the jar. Carried by the tiny current, the plankton clustered against the edge of the glass.

In a way the jar was a microcosim of the crater. Too round of course, and it needed the rocky jutting of islands and cities here and here and here and here. The Highisle, Arnar, Brokenfoot, and shadowy Perseverance. The *Lunglance* would be about here, creeping slowly along the northern margin of the crater; aboard it, the tiny fleck of protoplasm that was John Newhouse, visible only with a microscope. A quaint conceit, I told myself. I went below and fell asleep. The ship sailed on.

Next morning there were faint stirrings in the dust. Desperandum was soon up, fishing delicately in the jar with a long-handled strainer made of woven string. Every few minutes he would pull out a twitching minnow or crablike anthropod and check off an egg on his list. Tinny bass humming came from his mask speaker. He was enjoying himself. I didn't like the look of the black webwork of stitches on his injured arm. The slash on his neck had healed well, but his arm was puffy and inflamed. I hoped he was taking antibiotics.

There was a discrepancy between the number of eggs on his list and the number of organisms he had been able to catch. It didn't seem to bother him. He could hardly expect to catch every animal just by fishing blindly with a strainer. After he had caught the same fish three times he shrugged good-naturedly and abandoned his efforts. It showed an unusual tolerance for frustration on Desperandum's part, and it surprised me. I had expected him to empty the whole tub through a net. Apparently he thought that might endanger the health of the specimens.

All in all he had caught sixteen specimens from twenty-eight eggs. On the next day he tried again. There were more nuggets of plankton now; their spores had been present when the dust was first added. Besides that, the other plankton, sensing the presence of water, had spawned. There were dozens of tiny nuggets, no larger than chips of glass. Some of the larger nuggets were missing. They had been eaten.

Desperandum added a little more water to promote the

growth of the major food source, then began fishing again. He had more success this time; he caught twenty specimens. Oddly, he was unable to catch some of the earlier specimens, including the fish he had caught three times yesterday. It didn't seem to bother him. After all, every creature there was entirely under his control.

I stopped my speculation. It was past my ability to fathom Desperandum's mental states; like all old people, he had passed into a different orientation, as different from my own as childhood is from adulthood.

We killed a whale that day and dumped three eggs overboard.

On the next day Desperandum caught only fifteen specimens. One of them was a small predatory octopus, which accounted for the disappearance of a few of the fish. Desperandum pulled it out of the tank and dissected it.

Twelve specimens on the next day. Desperandum rid himself of three omnivorous fish, assuming that they were the culprits. On his checklist he had correlated twenty-seven of the twenty-eight eggs. The shiny, spiny, black one remained unidentified.

When he found only four specimens on the day after that Desperandum grew annoyed. He emptied out the jar. Dust rustled sluggishly across the deck and flowed under the rail into the sea. Desperandum quickly rescued the specimens that lay struggling or scuttling on the deck; three crabs, a small vegetarian octopus, and the larva of a dust strider. He frowned. All of his captives ate nothing but plankton or, when they could get it, the long linked ropes of kelp common in this part of the crater.

Then he turned to the jar. There, stuck to the side of the glass with a dust-colored suction disk, was a small Nullaquan anemone.

"Astonishing!" Desperandum said aloud. "An anemone. What a stroke of luck."

The anemone looked quite healthy, as might be expected when it need only reach out one of its thorny arms for prey. It had eight arms, long, supple, pale brown tentacles studded with nastily sharp black thorns, like the branches of a rosebush. Each thorn was hollow, as were the

125

arms; each thorn was a sucking, vampirish beak. The arms sprouted from a short, thick trunk; at the bottom of the trunk was a snaillike suction foot. At the junction of the arms was a complicated pink arrangement of layers, not unlike the petals of a flower. Like a flower, it was a genital organ. The anemone was quite strong for a creature of its size. It's foot-long tentacles waved freely even without the support of the dust. It breathed through the siphonlike tips of its arms; they were thin, so it was not surprising that they had never been noticed.

The anemone seemed disturbed by the loss of its dust. It waved its tentacles indecisively, and finally hooked one over the rim of the jar. Then it released its suction hold on the glass with a faint pop and began to pull itself slowly and laboriously up the side of the glass.

"Dust! Quickly!" Desperandum snapped, watching the anemone with all the concern of a devoted parent for a sick child. Soon a crewman arrived with a bucket, and Desperandum poured it slowly into the tub. "More, more," Desperandum demanded impatiently. Soon the level of the dust swirled up to one of the anemone's slowly threshing tentacles. The plantlike animal released its hold and slipped into the dust, almost gratefully, it seemed to me.

Desperandum noticed my attention. "They're extremely rare," he told me. "I'd heard that there was a last colony of them living in the bay northwest of here, but I'd never seen one. No wonder I couldn't account for that last egg." Desperandum laughed jovially. He was enjoying himself.

I hoped that his new pet wouldn't bite him. The way it had tried to climb out of its jar struck me as ominous. I would hate to wake up some night and pry its barbs away from my throat.

Next day I climbed up on deck after leaving the breakfast dishes for Dalusa. I found Desperandum standing beside the glass urn, holding a wiggling spratling over the dust. Hesitantly, a brown, barbed arm lifted from the opacity and wrapped itself around the fish. The fish flapped weakly a few times and then stiffened. Testing the anemone's strength, Desperandum kept a firm grip on the fish's dry gray tail. Soon another tentacle snaked upward out of the dust; Desperandum snatched his fingers back just before the second tentacle lashed out at his hand. The fish disappeared under the surface.

"Strong little monster!" Desperandum said admiringly. "They were all over the crater before it was settled, you know. They kept attacking ships, innocently enough, and poisoned themselves. One sip of human blood through one of those thorn-beaks killed them almost instantly. I'd even heard that they were extinct. No one would visit their last stronghold up north for fear of mutual destruction. Perhaps they're making a comeback."

Wonderful, I thought. A few hundred camouflaged killers would add spice to the Nullaquan existence. I wondered how large the creatures grew. Ten feet? Perhaps as much as twenty? There appeared the image of a venomous monster as big as a sequoia, biding its time in the dry black darkness beneath the ship. One massive barbed tentacle wrapped around the *Lunglance,* a negligent tug, and there would be another quick addition to the mysteries of the sea. Hunger would be too strong a motive; why, mere curiosity would be abundantly fatal.

Dalusa spotted a pod of dustwhales that day, but by the time the *Lunglance* reached the spot they had vanished.

The anemone continued to grow. Desperandum prudently put a weighted iron grating on top of the urn. The crewman gave the jar a wide berth whenever possible, especially when the creature would stick its barbed appendages out into the open air and wiggle them energetically. As it grew, the anemone was growing darker; now its arms were the color of dried blood.

When young Meggle came in for the officers' lunch at noon, he told me sullenly that the captain wanted to see me. I reported to the cabin after a suitable lapse of time. Desperandum was just finishing his meal.

We went to the cabin; Desperandum ostentatiously shut the door. "I suppose you must have heard the rumor that I'm thinking of heading the ship for Glimmer Bay."

That was the reputed home of the last anemones. "Yes, I've heard it," I lied decisively.

"What do you think of it?" he said.

I felt that his frankness called for an evasion on my part. "I'd like to hear your reasons for going first."

"Very well. It concerns the specimen, of course. I'd like to keep it on board and study its habits, perhaps donate it later to the Church Zoo in the Highisle. On the other hand, it would be unethical to deprive an endangered species of a potential member of its gene pool. I'd have to see the situation for myself, take a census of the anemone population. Of course, that could be inconvenient."

The captain did not seem inclined to go further. He leaned back in his swivel chair and steepled his blunt, broad fingers.

"Let's count up the advantages and disadvantages of each course of action," I said at last. "First, the case against going. It's out of our way and will lengthen the voyage. It's a voyage into essentially unexplored territory, with danger from shoals and currents. And the *Lunglance* might be attacked by anemones."

"There's not really much danger in that," Desperandum interrupted mildly. "Even at their heyday the largest known anemone was only thirty feet long. Not large enough to menace the ship as a whole."

"We might lose a crew member, though."

"Possible. And you've left out a hazard. Glimmer is a very small bay, almost completely landlocked. The sun shines there for only about an hour a day. The gloominess and the walls are said to cause acute depression, melancholia, claustrophobia, even for the native Nullaquan."

I lifted my brows.

"Oh, it's quite plausible," Desperandum said. "Have you ever visited Perseverance?"

"No, sir."

"I have, of course. It's quite depressing there, too; it's built half a mile up the cliff on the western side of a narrow bay, with an unpleasant climate and an overwhelming sense of the presence of thousands of miles of solid rock. I have little doubt that the choice of that site as a center of religion and government has had a profound effect on the Nullaquan character." Desperandum sighed and folded his hands over his stomach.

"Well, then, sir, considering the advantages of this side trip," I said, when an uncomfortable silence had hobbled by on crippled feet. "I can only think of two. First, knowledge about the anemone population; second, a decision as to what to do with your little specimen. Now, as I see it, the first one involves danger to both the crew and the wildlife. And as for the second, well, it depends on the rarity of the specimens. And since you caught one in a single day, with a single net, I can hardly believe that they are really very rare.

"And one last thing. We're approaching Perseverance now. It would be simple to stop there and consult the Church about mounting a special expedition."

Desperandum looked at me stonily. "I tried that four years ago. They listened politely and then asked me for my Academy diploma."

I thought about apologizing and decided against it. It would have only have heightened the captain's sense of inferiority, his resentment at his lack of legitimate status. "Your arguments are good, but I'm not convinced," Desperandum said. "We will explore the bay."

I had expected as much.

The crew showed no surprise when ordered to sail north, tacking against the wind. Theirs was not to reason why. Besides, by this time they were probably incapable of it.

Later, I leaned on the starboard rail and looked at the tier after tier of ridged and battered rock that rose and rose in ragged rows to the planet's surface. It was a dry, bright morning, like all Nullaquan mornings. The monotony irritated me. A blast of freezing wind, a thick fog, or a savage hailstorm would have been a relief. My sinuses were giving me trouble; my chapped and itchy hands were slick with some unpleasant lotion that the first mate had given me. I didn't like the lotion much. Below in the kitchen, where I could remove my mask, it stank.

I heard the rasp of thorns on an iron grating. The anemone had been growing quickly on Desperandum's pampering diet, as if it were only too eager to reach breeding age and help in its species' promised comeback. It seemed

129

cramped in its jar and pulled repeatedly on its grating, as if building up its strength.

Dalusa was out on patrol, trying to locate the narrow inlet into Glimmer Bay. Desperandum navigated using aerial maps of the crater, made by the original colony ship. They were five hundred years old. Glimmer Bay had not even existed then.

I saw Dalusa come winging in from the north-northwest. She alighted neatly in the crow's nest, honked her horn to alert the crew, and then leapt into space. She fell in a neat parabola, opening her wings and with a snap just before breaking her ribs on the rail. She enjoyed that.

Dalusa flew swiftly away until she was a white speck against the dark background of cliff. There she caught a thermal and circled as the *Lunglance* tacked sluggishly after her.

When we reached an immense promontory of fallen rock, Dalusa swept gracefully around it, out to sea. Suddenly she shot southwards, flapping energetically but making no more headway than a swimmer in a rip tide. It was a wind, a strong one. Dalusa wheeled to face it. She still made no headway, but began to gain height. The ship sailed nearer. I was able to see a thin, sleeting fog now, at the dust-air interface. There were no waves.

Dalusa seemed to be tiring. She kept gaining height, but now she was losing ground out to sea.

Suddenly she entered an area of calm. She slowed her climb, but was then caught by another wind, equally powerful but blowing in the opposite direction. She backed against it, tried to turn, looped sickeningly when she hit a patch of turbulence. Wind tore at the loose dress that was all she wore.

Recovering, Dalusa shut her wings and dropped. She gained speed, corrected her trajectory slightly in mid-fall, then opened her wings and swooped toward the ship. She had judged the windspeed beautifully. She faced the edge of the promontory. She faced it—there had always been something a little odd about the structure of her neck. The two vectors, correcting one another, sent her gliding toward the ship. She made it, soared gracefully over the port

130

rail, and collapsed silently on the deck in a wing-shrouded heap.

Mr. Flack was at her side in an instant. He extended a hand to touch her shoulder, remembered in time, and drew back. Dalusa's long thin arms trembled with fatigue. She had hidden her face—her mask, actually—under one wing. Flack could do nothing for her. His medical knowledge did not extend to nonhumans.

"Get the lady a pallet," Flack said harshly. "Water. Rest."

The doctor's panacea for those beyond his comprehension. I took a blanket from our harpooneer, Blackburn, wrapped it carefully around Dalusa, and lifted her effortlessly. She weighed perhaps forty pounds, that was mostly muscle. Dalusa's pale shapely legs were mostly decoration. They had the texture of human flesh—more or less— but they were no denser than cork.

I carried Dalusa down to the kitchen, turned my pallet over so that no residual contamination could reach her, and set her down. She pulled her mask off.

"I'm all right," she said. "You shouldn't have troubled yourself." She immediately fell asleep.

There was nothing more to be done. I went back on deck.

We rounded the promontory. The wind caught us immediately; there was a sandpaper rattle of particles on the bow. The sails filled, the braces strained tight, and the *Lunglance* actually listed, a surprising feat for a trimaran of her bulk. Desperandum wore ship and started on a starboard tack.

North, there was a huge gap in the rock. Five hundred years ago there had been a narrow cliff there, separating the Nullaqua Crater from a minor subcrater that was now Glimmer Bay. There had been a crack in that cliff. The Glimmer Crater, receiving sunlight only at noon, was much colder than the parent crater. A cold draft developed, laden with abrasives. Soon a small natural arch formed, housing a vertical whirlwind, hot air above, cold below. Over two centuries, the arch expanded.

On the two hundred and thirty-seventh year of human

settlement on Nullaqua, the cliff collapsed with a report heard throughout the crater. It was insufficient warning. Thousands of tons of rock fell into the sea, and the resulting tsunami wiped out almost the entire Nullaquan fleet. Five ships survived: three fishing ships accidentally sheltered by the Highisle, a single retired Arnarian warship in the Pentacle Islands, and a whaler from Brokenfoot. There were no surviving ships from Perseverance. Perseverance had been razed a year earlier in the Nullaquan Civil War.

The year after the Glimmer Catastrophe was known as the Hungry Year.

The *Lunglance* headed as closely into the wind as possible. Mr. Bogunheim was at the tiller; the sails luffed a little and Captain Desperandum chided the man absently. The captain was gazing into the dim recesses of the bay, his binoculars pressed tightly to the lenses of his dustmask.

Films of dust were forming in the wind shadows of objects on deck. The anemone rattled its bars. I wondered if it recognized our location. Like one of those homing birds, widgets, pidgets, some name like that . . .

It was after noon now. Dim light filtered into the bay from two sources, the entrance, two miles wide, and a glowing sliver of hills at the eastern part of the crater. An immense ridge of dark rock blocked most of the afternoon light that shone on the hills beyond. It was as dim, as gloomy as the interior of a shuttered cathedral. There was a churchlike atmosphere inside. The *Lunglance* soon passed the bordering guardian cliffs and sailed eastward in the hushed, weak wind.

Behind us an immense vertical beam of pale light, fifty miles high, shone through the mouth of the bay and across to the broken, battered cliff wall. It was sublime in the extreme. Everyone on deck, with the exception of Desperandum, stared, completely rapt, at the dim colossus of light. It glowed like the promise of redemption.

I tore my eyes away and shivered. It was as cold and gloomy as the bottom of a well in Glimmer Bay, but dry. Dessicated. Mercilessly dry, drier than the driest desert on Earth, Bunyan, or Reverie, dry enough to make one's nose split and bleed at night, dry enough to make one's hair crackle with static electricity, dry enough to make sparks sting one's knuckles over and over again. It stole the water from my mouth, the tears from my eyeballs.

And cold. The men got out their night gear and put it on. Nullaquan nights were cold; here they would be much worse.

Hot air coming into the bay cooled by expansion; cold air replaced it. There was a faint, shuddery draft in Glimmer Bay, like the breath of a beast with lungs of ice. Dry ice.

The beam behind us gave no heat. The narrowness of the channel caused it to be absolutely stationary; the sun's movement would have no effect on it except to change its brightness. The lowest part of the beam was slightly fuzzy with dust mist; the beam grew fainter with height as the air grew thinner and clearer. Eventually the beam vanished, but the light itself still made the airless cliff wall glow with a dim vacuum radiance, forty miles away.

At sea level, the entire bay was a rough oval, fifty miles long, twenty-six miles across. The inlet was located at about the middle of the bay.

We sailed east. It grew dimmer; many times the sailors turned to stare regretfully at the light behind us.

Now the captain decided to conduct a test for the presence of anemones. Under his orders the crew scampered up the ratlines and furled the sails. Desperandum heaved a dust drag overboard, then threw out an immense gutted chunk of shark meat. A wired-on float kept it from sinking.

The meat began to drift slowly from the ship. There were no signs of questing tentacles. Perhaps it was too deep for the creatures. A dust strider came skating creakily up out of the distance on saucer-shaped feet. He began to chew thoughtfully on the meat. The diet of adult striders differed from that of their larvae. The strider found the meat acceptable and was soon joined by a dozen relatives, skating up rapidly out of the gloom like roaches after a forgotten crumb. Desperandum grew impatient; he pulled the shark meat back on board. The striders clung to it tenaciously. Desperandum dropped the meat to the deck with a thump and the striders scattered, but not for long. Brushed aside,

133

they returned single-mindedly to the meal. Desperandum finally had to swat one of their number with a whaling spade, whereupon the rest scuttled energetically away and leapt overboard.

There was not much plankton here; the light was too scarce. The Glimmer Bay ecology must be based on carrion washed in by the currents, I thought. The light was growing dimmer ahead of us as the sun sank. Desperandum set out lanterns.

The light was welcome, but it seemed almost a profanation of the titanic gloom and stillness. I felt uncomfortably conspicuous. The lights were like a shouted challenge to whatever denizens lived in this stagnant backwater, this nasty little rock coffin. I didn't like this place. I didn't like the black, looming cliffs, going up and up and up until they seemed taller than God. Those cliffs seemed eager to give in under their own massive weight, to slump together into the narrow gloom-choked bay and flatten the *Lunglance* like a bug between two bricks. I didn't like the cold and the silence.

I decided to go below and start work on the day's last meal. As I turned to go I glanced over the rail.

The dimness was speckled with hundreds of little red sparks. It was the reflection of lamplight in the multifaceted eyes of an incredible horde of dust striders. The *Lunglance* was surrounded by the little beasts, silently watching our lamps with the devotion of moths for a candle.

It must be a spawning ground, I thought. They could flatten themselves and ride the currents into the bay, then rush back out after breeding, skipping lightly across the dust with the wind at their backs.

More appeared even as I watched. They were thick for yards in every direction. The first mate engaged Desperandum in rapid conversation. The captain looked over the rail and shrugged.

The striders grew agitated. Panic spread through the packed thousands; they began to jump up and down lightly like water droplets on a red-hot griddle. They were going into a frenzy. I was disquieted. It was a good thing that the rail was four feet above the water. The spidery little monsters, six inches across, were leaping energetically upwards, but the deck was out of their reach.

Then they started to climb atop one another, careless of life, smothering the weak underfoot in the dust, inspired to some inexplicable peak of insectine fanaticism by the unwonted stimulus of light. Soon the first dozens were over the side, scuttling insanely across the deck, running in circles, falling onto their backs and kicking their spiny, saucered legs frantically. The men drew back indecisively as the creatures poured onto the deck. I also began to withdraw. I passed the anemone's jar; with a cunning whiplash movement it almost managed to sink its black hook-thorns into the back of my neck.

Slowly, not seeming to realize it, the men were forced into the dimmest area of the deck, behind the mizzenmast and close to the hatch that led to the captain's cabin and the hold.

Suddenly one of the creatures leapt up and sank its multiple mandibles into Mr. Grent's calf. He yelped with pain. That did it; the men went berserk, and soon the pattering rattle of little cup-shaped feet was joined by the brittle crunching of striders mashed underfoot.

Desperandum gave orders, bellowing so loudly that his mask speaker shrieked with distortion: "Get below, men! I'll handle this!"

The captain bounced across the deck to the nearest lantern and shut it off. With a few final vindictive dance steps the men began to file through the hatch. Desperandum, brushing bugs off his legs, headed for the second lantern. I stepped nimbly onto half a dozen hapless striders and ducked through the kitchen hatch. I slammed it behind me and felt my way down the stairs to the light switch.

There were two striders on the kitchen floor. I flattened them with a saucepan and started cooking.

Mr. Flack spread ointment on the bites of the crewmen. That night the men ate in the hold. They slept there, too, as the striders showed no inclination to leave the ship. We peeked up every half hour; the lantern invariably drew an eager horde of light-crazy striders. They seemed determined to set up housekeeping.

The captain showed no concern. "They'll tire, men," he told the crew as, preparing to sleep, they nestled uncomfortably in their blankets. "And if they don't tomorrow we'll drive them off. We have plenty of whale oil; we'll go up with torches and burn them out."

The men looked cheered at this. Personally, I suspected that the plastic-clad deck was highly flammable. I foresaw the ship in a sheet of flame. The stored water in the hold would make a magnificent bloom in Glimmer Bay; but no one would ever see it.

But my fears were unfounded. Next morning, the light from the inlet slowly shamed the few wretched stars in our limited sky into hiding their faces, then turned the darkness into slate gray shadow. A splinter of light showed on the western rim of the crater behind us. It grew to a glow.

The striders liked their new home. They were getting along famously. Doubtless any novelty was welcome here. With morning they seemed much calmer, they were even magnanimous enough to tolerate a few sailors on deck. They bore no grudges.

Taking advantage of their good nature, Desperandum spread a thick pool of raw whale oil onto the deck on the port side of the ship, between the foremast and the mainmast. A faint breeze bore the odor along the ship; soon the striders came clicking across the deck to investigate. They approved. They were silent, but they pantomimed their appreciation thoroughly, wading through the shadow, cozy stuff and slurping it into their complicated, chitinous mouths. A few of them even danced like bees.

Desperandum waited at a distance, patiently, holding a pipe lighter in one massive hand. The oil was slowly spreading. Now the striders were trampling one another in their urge to get at the juice, with that lack of fraternal concern that seemed to be their trademark. They scampered in eagerly from all over the ship.

"Issue whaling spades to take care of any survivors," Desperandum said calmly lighting a strip of cloth. He tossed it neatly into the center of the pool of oil.

It went up with a roar. The striders began to scream, high-pitched *ee-ee-ee* sounds like rusty meat griders. They caught like tinder. A few of them even exploded, showering their brethren with the flaming contents of their stomachs. Striders ran desperately across the deck, faltered, and crumpled, their smoldering legs splitting and spitting over-heated juices. Some made it over the rail to the sea, and ran screeching along the surface, trailing fire.

The men began to kill the rest with the flat sides of their whaling spades. Each flattened strider left a smoldering patch on the deck. The plastic under the puddle of oil had melted a little; charred bits of strider exoskeleton were stuck in its cooling surface, but it had not caught fire.

The last screeches were cut off suddenly by the efficient crunching of spades.

"Good work, men," said Captain Desperandum. He was all satisfaction. "Weigh drag. Jump lively aloft and loose the sails, and let them hang in the clews and bunts."

The men did this. I was turning below to prepare lunch when I heard it.

Ee-ee-ee-ee-ee.

From the east, from the dry, dead dimness at the dust-washed base of the cliffs, came an astounding host of strid-ers. The twilit surface of the bay was black with them, close-packed millions scuttling furiously toward the *Lunglance.* The tepid winds could never bear us away in time. The hideous little vermin were moving so fast that their saucered feet sent up puffs of dust.

They moved like a million tightly wound clockwork roaches.

Desperandum walked calmly to the stern to observe the advancing multitude. At that moment the sun appeared, edging slowly over the rim of the bay. The effect of direct sunlight was immeasurably cheering. The bay was brighter, airier place, less reminiscent of open graves, abandoned mine shafts, and similar unpleasant places. The striders were changed from an unnerving menace to a mere irrita-tion.

"Get below and fetch me a barrel of oil," Desperandum said. Three crewmen, one of them Murphig, hurried below and were soon back, groaning under their ivory burden. Desperandum picked up the barrel and held it casually under one arm as he walked to the stern railing. He touched the catch with one foot and folded the railing down. The striders were closing fast now, showing no fear of the sudden sunlight, their faceted eyes glittering like cheap imitation rubies.

Desperandum peeled off the barrel's watertight whaleskin top and started to pour the oil overboard in a thick stream. Having never before poured whale oil on dust, he was unaware of its peculiar properties. It did not spread out in a thin flammable film, as he had expected. Instead it soaked up dust in a thick black cake and sank like a rock.

I could not see Desperandum's expression because of his dustmask, but I imagine that he was aghast. The creatures were almost on us now; their rusty creaking was deafening.

Desperandum set the barrel down. "Get below!" he shouted. The men stood stunned for a second, then rushed for the hatches.

The striders surrounded us now, trampling one another in their eagerness to get on deck. There were not as many as I had first thought. Perhaps there were as few as a million. Still making a head-hurting noise like metal files on one's own teeth, they began to swarm up under the railing. The ship was still moving; this gave them some difficulty. Desperandum was trying to rescue his anemone. It seemed to resent rescue and kept him at bay with snaps of its tentacles. They were as effective as threats of suicide.

Another day cramped in the hold was more than I could bear. I had been enjoying the sunlight. Nullaqua's sun, usually more tinged with blue than I thought aesthetically necessary in a star, had never looked so beautiful. Besides, Dalusa was out on patrol and I wanted to wait for her. So, as the rest of the crew ducked through the hatches, I sprang energetically into the ratlines and climbed up several feet above the deck. My head was on a level with the mainsail yard.

Desperandum was still fiddling with his specimen. Now he was cut off from both of the hatches in the center hull. Worst of all, his specimen did not need any of his help, if I could judge by the sixteen drained strider corpses I had found outside its urn that morning.

Desperandum was surrounded. Suddenly the faithful Flack stuck his dustmasked head out of the kitchen hatch. "Captain! Captain, this way!" he shouted, but his voice was barely audible over the intolerable screeching. Nevertheless, Desperandum looked up.

Something thudded gently against the side of the ship.

The screeching stopped, cut off short and unanimously. My ears rang with silence. As one, the striders leapt off the starboard side of the ship, and, in panic-stricken silence, began to skate off at top speed across the dust.

It was one of the most extraordinary things I had ever seen.

Then came something that made it pale into insignificance.

Over the port railing came an immense tapering tube the size of a young tree trunk, studded with layered rosebush thorns at least six inches in diameter. It was followed by the rest of a sluggishly weaving nest of tentacles, black, thorned atrocities thick enough to use for water mains. I didn't get a very good look as I was too busy panicking and running up the ratline.

By the time I had caught my breath, the new anemone had ensconsed itself comfortably between the mainmast and the mizzenmast, and it showed every sign of willingness to make its stay permanent.

It was a full-grown specimen, I noted from my somewhat shaky position on the main lower topgallant yard. Its tentacles were a good twenty-five feet long; its barrel body perhaps four feet high, a little over five feet if one counted its immense, rather discolored rose. It looked fat and happy, reminiscent somehow of a well-fed Nullaquan. It had seven tentacles; the eighth had apparently been chewed off in some childhood mishap.

It languidly draped three of its tentacles across the topsail braces and the main brace, wrapping them securely like grapevine tendrils around the wires of a trellis. The inner and outer lifts of the yard beneath my feet sang with tension. I immediately abandoned it and headed for the crow's nest.

A questing tentacle found the mainmast and tugged at it.

139

The entire thing shook; I clung with cramped fingers to the ratline.

For a moment the idea had struck me that the anemone had boarded us to rescue its captive offspring. That notion was dispelled a few moments later when, with a negligent sweep of one arm, the anemone knocked the glass jar from its table. It hit the deck with a crash and a clang.

The heavy iron grating had crushed two of the young anemone's tentacles; a shard of glass had stabbed its tubular body. It dragged itself with crippled slowness across the deck.

Somehow the anemone sensed movement. With unerring accuracy it picked its young kinsman from the deck and tasted it with a neat thorn puncture just above the suction foot. It found cannibalism less than appealing and dropped its victim to the deck with a complete lack of interest. Deeply wounded, perhaps mortally, the young anemone crawled painfully to the rail, trailing yellowish juice. It fell overboard and sank without a trace.

The situation was critical. One of the anemone's long thorny tentacles was laid neatly on top of the kitchen hatch. Another was within easy striking range of the tiller. It would be very difficult to change course. Worse yet, in another hour or so we would crash into a nasty-looking fanged promontory, dead ahead. We *had* to tack.

Now the hatch to the captain's cabin snapped open and half a dozen crewmen came up to join Desperandum. One of them was Flack, the first mate. He and Desperandum held a hurried consultation. Desperandum shook his head. His objection was obvious. He had seen the injury of his once-captive anemone; now this leathery monster might be the last of its kind. It was not to be harmed.

The anemone was quiet now; three tentacles clinging to the braces, four others sprawled limply across the deck. If it stretched hard it might be able to reach the hatch to the captain's cabin, but it had apparently gone to sleep. The lack of a supporting medium did not seem to bother it. I looked north. A faint dust cloud marked the path of the striders, still in full retreat. Beyond that, bright sunlight showed a distance-shrunken figure winging our way. It was Dalusa.

I felt uncomfortable in the rigging. I decided to descend, very carefully, while the anemone was still quiet.

Most of the crew had joined the captain by now. He was still discussing tactics with his three mates. The crew stood marveling; three of them nervously clutched whaling spades, and Blackburn had one of his harpoons. I began to creep quietly down the ratline. The anemone showed no sign of noticing me.

I was almost within dropping distance of the deck when Desperandum saw me.

"Newhouse!" he shouted. His cry alerted both of us, but the anemone reacted faster. A tentacle swung up off the deck like the boom of a crane, directly at me. I don't know how I did it, but seconds later I found myself poised perilously on the footrope of the main lower topsail yard, clutching the lifts for balance with rope-burned hands.

"Watch your step, Newhouse!" Desperandum admonished loudly. "You might have poisoned it!"

Maritime protocol could not have stifled my retort, but my mask was still on. I soon had my trembling under control. "As long as you're up there, Newhouse, start furling the sails. We have to reduce our speed or we'll hit the rocks."

Interspecies aggression was not my forte but I could see any number of simpler solutions to our problem. I made something of a botch job of furling the sails. It didn't help much, anyway, as I could only work four of them and the *Lunglance* had twenty.

Dalusa flapped nearer. She was flying low, and therefore, she was nearly grabbed by a cunning snap of tentacles. My heart leapt into my mouth. I swallowed with difficulty, returning it to its proper anatomical position. Human blood was reputed to kill anemones; I accepted that, although I did not care to put it to the test. But Dalusa's was different. She might be lethal, deadly even to Nullaquan sharks whose heavy-duty digestive systems made hors d'oeuvres out of human beings. On the other hand, the anemone might find her eminently delectable, even as I did.

141

The anemone seemed restless. It was not often that it got a chance at a tidbit like Dalusa, and the lost opportunity must have annoyed it. Rather pettishly, I thought, it wrapped two of its tentacles around the mainsail yard and ripped it loose with a snap. Another tentacle grabbed the young anemone's table, tugged it free from the deck, and threw it. The men scattered and the anemone, sensing movement, reached for them. Its arms stretched a surprising distance, so close to the hatch that several of the men abandoned that means of escape and leapt with commendable energy into the rigging.

While the anemone was distracted I streaked down the ratline, ignoring my injured hands, and ducked into the kitchen hatch. And just in time, too; as I shut it behind me a tentacle descended on it with such force that a thorn punched through the thin metal with a terrific report.

I dodged through the storeroom to the captain's dining room. Desperandum, surrounded by crewmen, was sitting on the table. It bowed under his weight.

"Fire would work. Harpoons would make short work of it. Killing it's no problem, it's at our mercy. What I want is some way to immobilize it."

The crew looked at him stonily. I pulled off my dustmask.

"I think that five good men could wrap it in a sail and have it completely trapped. Do I have any volunteers?"

I lifted my hand to wipe the sweat off my forehead.

"Not you, Newhouse. I need you to cook." He looked at me kindly, his small, wrinkle-shrouded eyes filled with appreciation. "No other volunteers?"

I broke in before the rest of the crew could be embarrassed by the revelation of their good sense.

"Captain, I have an idea."

"And that is?"

"We might drug the creature. A minimal dose of human blood should reduce its ability to resist."

"Drug it?"

"Yes, Captain. Drug." He looked so blank that I continued, "Drugs. Foreign chemicals introduced into its bloodstream."

142

"I know the meaning of the word, yes. That sounds practicable. Crewman Calothrick, bring a basin. I've been meaning to have this lanced, and this looks like a convenient time."

Calothrick still had his mask on, doubtless to hide his features, frozen in a Flare-blasted grin. By the time he returned with a basin, Desperandum had rolled up the sleeve of his white blouse and unwrapped a long stained bandage on his arm. The amount of infection and inflammation on that single arm would have put two or three lesser men to bed. Flack, lancet in hand, stared at the wound, then at the captain, as if expecting him to drop dead of blood poisoning on the spot. Desperandum refused to collapse, however, and at last Flack made a tentative puncture. I could tell by the crew's intake of breath. I had averted my eyes; infection disgusted me.

When the ordeal was over, Desperandum poured the loathsome fluids into a thin black plastic bag and sealed it with a twist of wire.

"I'll have Dalusa fly overhead and bomb the creature from a height," he said. "That flower petal arrangement it has looks vulnerable, wouldn't you say, Mr. Flack?"

Flack said, "Yes, sir. Have you a fever?"

"When I need medical help I'll request it. Fresh bandages."

"Needs open air, sir."

"I don't want any dust on it. Besides, it would stick to my sleeve." That was undoubtedly true. "Open that hatch a little, crewman. Lively now."

The man nearest the hatch opened it a tentative crack.

"Peek out. You see any of its tentacles nearby?"

"No, sir, I—"

The hatch was slammed instantly shut from the outside, rapping the crewman on the head so that he fell stunned down three stairs into the arms of crewman Murphig.

I looked up at the hatch. There were no thorn holes in it. That was lucky for the stunned crewman, as he had just escaped an instant trepanation.

"That settles that, then," Desperandum said. "The creature has shifted position. It can't reach both hatches at once. Mr. Bogunheim, go to the kitchen hatch and call the lookout in."

"Take your mask," I said. "The anemone punched a hole through the hatch just before I left." The dust-repelling electrostatic field cut off automatically when the hatch was shut, and even now dust was doubtless percolating downwards into the air in the hull.

Bogunheim returned in a few moments with Dalusa. She stared rather blankly at the supine figure of the stunned crewman, now being ministered to by Flack.

"Here," Desperandum said, handing her the black bag of blood. "I want you to fly over the anemone and bomb it with this. Try to be accurate, Dalusa."

"What is contained?" Dalusa asked, shaking the bag.

"Water," Desperandum said, lying so convincingly that I almost did a double take. "While you were aloft, did you notice the creature's latest position relative to the hatches?"

"Yes, Captain. It had three of its arms over by this hatch—" she pointed with a dramatic flare of wing—"but the other was unguarded."

"Fine. The men will be equipped with spades and nets. We will exit through the kitchen hatch and surround the specimen. Any actions taken will be strictly in self-defense and will involve the least amount of harm possible to the specimen. Try not to let it catch you. Remember your blood will poison it."

The men seemed eager to obey this order.

I went up on deck, armed with a spade, beside Calothrick. In desperate circumstances I thought it would be easier to kill the monster by feeding it Calothrick than by stabbing it to death. Any creature as simply constituted as an anemone would be hard to kill.

I had high hopes that the blood in Desperandum's bag would be an overdose. Poison would work, as long as Dalusa believed Desperandum's lie and carried out her job. I wondered if she had smelled the blood inside when she had her mask off. I had never asked her about the keenness of her sense of smell. What would she do if she knew it was blood? Bathe in it, thereby blistering off her entire skin sur-

144

face, or perhaps sip it, scorching her gullet and earning almost certain death from bacterial infestation?

But it was all beside the point now. Dalusa sculled swiftly upward on skin-taut, bat-furred wings and dropped the bag with a nasty splatter right onto the rosebud trunk junction of the anemone's limbs.

The anemone waved its tentacles indecisively as a gruel of clotting blood trickled down its trunk. Then it vomited, ejecting a thick yellow paste from the hollow tips of its thorn beaks. The paste squished nastily as it squeezed out; the noise lasted about five seconds.

Then the anemone stopped retching and, with apparent finickiness, flicked its arms and spattered the crew with its paste. A glob barely missed my head. Most of the crew, however, had been hit, as they had been closing in on the beast, with commendable courage. Disconcerted by the barrage of filth, they fell back in confusion. The anemone unstuck itself from the deck, threw out four tentacles, and dragged itself loopily through a group of crewmen. One alert sailor threw a net over the creature, which it promptly stole as it slid overboard to disappear beneath the dust.

Two of its breathing siphons appeared a dozen yards from the ship, each spitting a plume of dust.

Desperandum wiped splattered filth from the lenses of his dustmask and looked over the side. "Good! We can still track it!" he shouted. "Lookout!"

Dalusa had disappeared.

"Lookout! Dalusa! Where is that woman?"

There was a crunch and a scream of metal. The impact of the collision threw me on my face. I rolled over next to a splatter of vomit.

"Hard about!" bellowed Desperandum. "Shoals!"

The rocks beneath the surface must have been smoothed by erosion, otherwise they would have punched a hole through our starboard hull. As it turned out, we were only dented, and we were able to make the middle of the bay by sunset. It came early here, at a little before one o'clock. Once again the beam from the bay's inlet was our only source of light.

Soon eighteen of our twenty-six crew members began to

complain of nausea, including the captain. It did not take Mr. Flack long to determine that the cause of the illness was some microorganism from the anemone. Wherever the vomit had spattered, the crewmen's skins were alive with clustered scarlet bumps. Those most severely affected began to run fevers. None of the sick men showed an appetite for dinner.

Except for Captain Desperandum. As young Meggle was ill, I brought in the officer's meals myself after helping the skeleton crew clean the deck. Desperandum was not badly afflicted. Only the fingers of his right hand had the rash, where he had wiped clean the spattered lens of his dustmask.

When I brought in the tray Desperandum was talking to Flack. Flack was stripped to the waist; the rash mottled his chest where the contagion had penetrated his thin shirt. His face was flushed, but his physician's duty to the crew kept him on his feet where a more sensible man would have gotten drunk and gone to sleep.

"Heard rumors of an allergy connected with anemones," said Flack. "If it clears up in a week or so we'll be all right. I'm not trained to treat forgotten diseases, though. Anemones have not been the vector of an illness for three hundred years. There are records in Perseverance, though, and better-trained personnel. I say we should sail there, quickly."

I lifted the lid from a shrimp casserole. Steam gushed upwards; Flack turned slightly green. It was one of Captain Desperandum's favorite dishes, but he dug in with a marked lack of enthusiasm and passed the dish to Mr. Grent. Bogunheim was on deck sick with the men, but Grent, like me, had been lucky.

"I agree," said Desperandum, picking up a fork left-handed. "We cannot risk the health of the crew. It's a bitter disappointment for me; I had intended to make a start on a full study. But shoals, the sickness, and the strider menace . . . I'll return sometime later. Soon though." Desperandum lifted a morsel to his lips and swallowed it with difficulty.

Flack closed his eyes. "Sir," he said faintly. "When we

146

reach Perseverance, medical clergy should look at your arm. These things can creep up on a man, sir. . . ."

Desperandum looked annoyed. He inflicted another mouthful of casserole on himself. "You are a fine medical officer," he said after he had caught his breath. "But you must realize that my own medical knowledge is extensive, and I was trained in a culture whose medical technology is several centuries ahead of your own. It is solely a question of will, you see, of teaching the body to obey. Over the years I have had some measure of success. Perhaps you would like something to eat."

Flack shuddered. "No sir. If I might be excused . . ."

"Certainly, Mr. Flack. I forget that you are a sick man." Desperandum was still eating, painfully, when I left.

Dalusa was not in the kitchen. Instead I found Calothrick there, rummaging through the cabinets in search of my private stock of Flare.

"Have you run out again?" I said.

Calothrick started, then turned and grinned nervously. "Yeah."

"I thought you were sick. You're supposed to be flat on your back on deck."

"Well, that . . . yeah . . ." Calothrick mumbled. I could almost hear gears mesh in his head as he decided to tell the truth. "I was hit all right, and I got part of the rash on my arm. But after I took a blast of Flare, it went away, and I had to rub it to bring it back. See?" He held out his thin freckled arm. The rash did not look very convincing to me, but Flack would probably chalk it up to Calothrick's off-world physique.

"So you've been relaxing on deck while the rest of the healthy ones are working overtime."

"Wouldn't you do the same thing? Death, give me a break, John."

It was a difficult question.

"Besides, everyone saw me take that first splatter. If I got well too soon they'd get suspicious."

I nodded. "A good point. Except that your being up and about is twice as suspicious. Get back on deck before Murphig sees you're missing."

"He'll just think I've gone down to the recycler to puke," Calothrick said. "Besides, like you said, he's too busy working to pay me much attention."

"Murphig is healthy?" I said. "I thought I saw him take a splatter right across the leg."

"No, he . . . well, I'm not sure if he did or not, come to think of it. Oh, here we go." Calothrick brightened as he pulled out a jug of Flare and sniffed it. He took a frightening dose and then pulled a plastic packet out from under his flared sailor's trousers. It was held to his skinny calf with elastic bands. He started filling it with Flare.

"I saw it," I said. "He was hit. You realize what this means? Murphig has that bottle of Flare, the stolen one. He's cured himself."

"Murphig one of us?" Calothrick said incredulously. "Can't be. He's too much of a jerk." Suddenly the packet began to overflow. "Look out!" I said. Calothrick stopped hastily and looked at the small beaded splash on the plastic counter top.

"But he's not an idiot; he'd do what you're doing, faking it. There must be some other explanation."

Calothrick strapped the packet back onto his leg. The Flare didn't seem to be affecting him as strongly as usual. By now a blast like that was probably only just enough to hold him together. "I'm awful hungry, man," he complained. "You got anything to eat?"

"Get back on deck and try to look weak," I said. "The starvation will help."

"Hey, thanks a lot," Calothrick said resentfully. Then he bent over and licked up the counter top puddle of Flare with his broad, spatulate tongue.

It seemed that he was hardly gone before Murphig came into the kitchen. He pulled off his mask; we eyed each other warily.

"You're looking well," he said at last.

"So are you."

"I thought I saw you hit."

"I know I saw you," I said. "How's the leg?"

"No worse than your neck."

"Listen, Murphig," I said patiently, "what's on your mind? Food not to your taste?"

"Let's quit fencing, Newhouse," Murphig said. (Were his eyewhites just the faintest shade of yellow? No.) "You were hit, and I was hit, and neither one of us is sick. Fine. So you know it's psychosomatic. Are you going to tell the captain about it?"

Confused, I kept silent.

"If Desperandum finds out he'll keep us in the stinking backwater until something eats us alive," Murphig said anxiously. "We're breaking custom to come here. We're begging for death, do you understand? This is their game preserve. The men know it. Even Desperandum knows it, somewhere inside, or else he wouldn't be sick. We're cracking . . . panicking. The longer we stay in here the worse the men will get."

He seemed to expect an answer. I nodded.

"Even your little winged friend, huh?" Murphig said nastily. "She's like a bird in a cage here. You know what birds are? Yeah, of course . . . I saw her crack right after she hit the anemone; she headed east for the shadows. If you don't get her out of here, she'll die. You have influence with the captain. Get us out."

"We're leaving already," I said. "And Dalusa, while no miracle of stability, is probably closer to sanity than you are."

Murphig thought that over. "Yes. I can see how an offworlder might think that."

"Murphig," I said, "get out of my kitchen before you make me break into hives."

"You and I will have to work double shifts until we get out of here and the crew heals up. But I suppose you know that."

"Out, Murphig!"

Murphig left.

The outrushing cold breeze at the mouth of Glimmer Bay had caught the *Lunglance*; with the wind directly at our backs, we made for the middle of the channel. It was a simple maneuver; the bay seemed to usher us back into the sunlight. Mr. Grent had taken the tiller; below, Desperandum and I conversed in his cabin.

"I've had to face a temporary defeat here, Newhouse," the captain said. "I can't say I like that much. I'd turn this bay upside down, plague or no plague, if I didn't know I'd be back. But I'll be here next year, I swear that. With a . . . well, did you ever hear of a helicopter?"

"Certainly."

"After this voyage I'll have one built—secretly. I'll run it on whale oil. I'll need a crewman."

"I don't know much about Nullaquan law, Captain, but isn't that illegal?"

"Why should that stop us?"

It was a good question. "Why a helicopter?"

"Because they're fast, mobile, and invulnerable. I'll take it on board ship—no one will recognize it for what it is, since there's not a Nullaquan alive that's ever seen a flying machine. Too wasteful of resources. But the *Lunglance* will stop outside the bay; we'll row off under cover of darkness and ride the updraft inside. Then, whatever's necessary . . . a few mild depth charges, for instance, should bring any anemones to the surface. I consider it a damn shame that I didn't get a population count. For all we know, those two were the only members of their species left on the planet."

I glanced past Desperandum's shoulder and out of the window in the stern. Behind us, outlined by the inpouring glow from the crater, came Dalusa. She looked tired; her wings moved slowly and laboriously, as if she had been flying all night.

"Only two, Captain? Unlikely. A fertilized egg in our nets implies at least two adults. Or are they hermaphroditic?"

"No. But solid proof, you see, an actual specimen or authenticated eyewitness account . . . well, they're lacking. We can't be rock-solid certain."

I gestured at the windows. "The lookout is coming in."

Desperandum glanced outwards. "That's good. I'll dock her pay for the time she missed."

An inch on his splattered hand distracted him. He ran one blunt finger gently over an inflamed knuckle.

We were halfway through the strait now, moving at a tremendous rate for the *Lunglance*. Behind us a strong gust caught Dalusa and she swooped low.

A forest of barbed tentacles leapt upwards from beneath the surface, scattering dust that trailed off, stolen by the wind. Dalusa beat desperately upwards; monster thorns scratched the air she had just vacated. As she gained height the anemones—a dozen at least—sank regretfully beneath the dust.

Desperandum was still fiddling with his knuckle. "Captain, did you see that?" I said.

"See what?" said Desperandum.

Chapter 13

A Conversation with a Young Nullaquan Sailor

The illness vanished almost immediately once we were out of Glimmer Bay. We did not go to Perseverance after all.

Three weeks into our fifth month at sea we discovered a pod of whales and slaughtered all day. I think we attracted upwards of two hundred sharks.

We butchered the whales more quickly than seemed humanly possible. Everyone was pressed into the effort. Even Desperandum wielded his mighty axe with the rest. The crew wore cleats on their shoes when they attached the hoisting hooks; a single slip would have sent them into the rending jaws of the sharks, and not even Desperandum's vindictive lance could have saved them in such an eventuality.

No matter how quickly we pulled our massive victims onto the deck, their bellies were still ripped to oozing tatters by the scavengers. Several of our men were grieviously bitten by pilot fish; one lost a finger. We hacked and butchered and hoisted all day, and the sulfurous fires of the try-pots were kept burning far into the night, staining our white sails with a thin coat of soot. At last the crew fell into their bunks like dead men.

Next morning Desperandum officially announced that the holds were full. The crew pulled off their masks for a brief moment to give a single cheer, then walked into the galley tent to settle down to a gala breakfast.

Despite the vastly increased workload that this day of celebration cost me, I was in a good mood. Dalusa, her scouting trips no longer necessary, worked hard at my side. After numerous false starts she was showing promise of becoming a talented cook. Besides that, I had four flasks of quality syncophine hidden securely in the kitchen, surely all that I could possibly smuggle off planet.

Later that night the crew began to drink heavily. It seemed that only one of us was not swept away by the holiday mood: Captain Desperandum. The captain had been sulking in his cabin for the past few days, perhaps ill from his arm, which had still not healed. I got stumbling drunk, and Dalusa went to talk to the captain. She never drank alcohol, and the sight of drunkenness made her uneasy. She could not accustom herself to the altered behavior patterns.

As we sailed on toward the Highisle it became obvious that something was occupying the captain's mind. Days passed, and the crew settled into a dumb torpor, whiling away the hours with scrimshaw. Not so Desperandum. He paced the triple deck restlessly, scanning the horizon. On one occasion he even climbed up to the crow's nest, though the mainmast groaned alarmingly under his weight.

On the morning of the seventh day we spotted another whale. To the surprise of everyone, Desperandum ordered the crew to pursue it. They were happy to do so; everyone aboard was suffocating with boredom. Desperandum called me to his side.

"I knew we'd find one more," he told me quietly. "I need this whale for science, Newhouse. For knowledge. For human dignity. I won't be kept in ignorance, you see. I can't allow it. I have to take this opportunity; I'll stake everything on it. You'll see, John."

As we drew closer to the whale Desperandum took one of the harpooneer's posts himself, although it was against all custom. "Steer as close to the monster as you can, men!" he shouted at us from behind the gun. "It has to be done with one shot."

Desperandum anointed his harpoon with his own blood and loaded the gun. The whale was unusually skittish; it sounded well before we were in range. Desperandum second-guessed it with uncanny accuracy, however, and it

153

surfaced almost under our bow. The captain aimed deliberately and fired into a weak spot between two sections of armor. The whale gave a single blood-choked shriek and dented the *Lunglance's* bow with its tail. Desperandum had fired with telling effect, and the creature died in less than a minute.

Desperandum lumbered across the deck and shouted, "Now, men! Haul it on board before the sharks can bite through its hide! But use the slings, not hooks. I don't want any more holes in the beast."

I had been wondering about those slings. Using them was slow and clumsy. But strangely, the sharks, which appeared in under five minutes, seemed less than enthusiastic. A trio of them swam alongside the *Lunglance*, just out of reach of our whaling spades. They seemed to be watching and waiting.

Desperandum did not give them a second thought. As soon as the whale was on deck he pulled out the harpoon with his own hands and began to give orders. The harpoon stab was lengthened into a six-foot slash in the animal's left side. The crew cut through the tough flesh and cartilage between two of the ribs and, under the captain's directions, they began to hollow out the creature, throwing its intestines overboard to the suspiciously languid sharks.

Desperandum pitched into the work with the eagerness of a total fanatic. When he rolled up his sleeves I saw that the long festering slash on his arm was finally healing.

It was exhausting work, and it ate up the rest of the day. I brooded on it after the rest of the crew had gone to sleep. It was not only the operations on the whale that bothered me. Several times I had seen Desperandum step back from the work to converse with Murphig. Murphig could not reply, of course, wearing his dustmask, but he certainly seemed to listen attentively.

It preyed on my mind. I couldn't sleep. I got up, dressed, put on my mask and crept quietly up the stairs for another look at the whale.

It was only a dim bulk in the starlight on the deck over our starboard hull. As I moved quietly between the sleeping tents I noticed the blurred glow of a lantern behind the

154

monster's flukes. I crept closer. Suddenly I heard something metallic bounce on the deck and roll off over the railing into the sea. The sound came from the other side of the whale. Silently, I ran forward and flattened myself against the shadowy side of the monster. As I moved cautiously toward the source of the light, I heard something that startled me: the sound of a real human voice, undistorted by speakers.

"You're going to give me some more of what was in that bottle."

It was Murphig's voice. I moved closer, crouching, till I could look over the flattened flukes of the dead dustwhale.

"I will not buy it," Murphig said tightly, and sneezed. He pressed his dustmask against his face and took a deep breath. There would be a trace of dust between the mask and his face, but his hairy nose could probably handle that. He had a harpoon in his other hand.

Calothrick's peeling mask hid his face, but I could see his fear from his posture. He had backed away a little and had his opened hands slightly spread before him, palms downward.

"My addiction was your responsibility. I'm not the fool you think I am . . . *off-worlder*." There was hatred in Murphig's voice. He took another breath; distorted shadows touched his face from the lantern on the deck. "You're as guilty as sin, you galactic." A breath. "Oblivion will take you. I want you to think of that." Breath. "*We* have achieved perfect stability. While you may live for hundreds of years you can't maintain the same personality, sinful as it is. We both know that in a few years you will manage to kill yourself. You will be dust, and less than dust. Even your culture will be rotten and forgotten. But we'll be alive and unchanged. And stable. For millions of years. Until the very sun goes out. And even then our ship is waiting. Do you see that little star up there? The one that moves? It's a small one. You probably never even noticed it. Oh, it's an old ship. Not like the kind you galactics ride. But it's still in orbit, waiting our call. Someday it will hold us again. And we'll still think the same things, and believe in the same God, and be the same people. And all of us will be remembered. Not like your people. And we'll find another planet, maybe your planet, after you are all dead. My descendants will dance on your ashes, Calothrick. If you live long enough to get back to that planet. Which you won't unless you give me more of that drug. That's the Confederacy's drug, isn't it? You don't have to say anything. I know it is. You alien parasite. Either you give it to me—" he shook his harpoon "—or it's through the guts and over the side for the sharks. Everyone will think you fell overboard."

The young Nullaquan sailor had grown hoarse over the last few sentences. The dust was affecting his throat. Suddenly he began to cough rackingly and pressed his dustmask to his face. He was still choking softly when Calothrick attacked him. The harpoon bounced off the whale and tumbled to the deck, and the mask flew from Murphig's palsied hand to land somewhere behind him. As the two grappled and fell to the deck Calothrick struck Murphig once, twice in the side with what looked like the open edge of his hand. Murphig squirmed aside, though, and got one foot braced against Calothrick's hip. He kicked out. Calothrick reeled back, hit the railing with the small of his back, overbalanced, and fell overboard without a word or even a muffled scream.

Immediately there came the sounds of sharks ripping him apart. That shocked me. I hadn't expected the sharks. They had expected Calothrick, though; and I knew the cold horror of their patience and their silent tryst with death.

Murphig was coughing his lungs out on the deck, on his hands and knees. He looked badly shaken. If he kept coughing he was going to wake the sailors. Then all hell would break loose; Murphig would probably confess everything.

I walked around the whale. Murphig didn't notice me until I handed him his mask. He pulled it on immediately. No doubt he had a lot to say to me, but he couldn't say it with his mask on. I indicated the kitchen hatch with one extended arm.

We walked to the kitchen hatch. Murphig walked half

bent, his arms wrapped around his sides. He seemed cold, or maybe he was stunned by the murder. We went down into the kitchen, Murphig first. I was carrying the lantern with the flame set low.

Murphig was still hugging his sides. I offered him the kitchen stool and he sat down, pulling off his mask with one hand. I sat on the counter top. Murphig's eyes were glazed yellow with Flare withdrawal. I took off my mask, and set the lantern on the counter by my side.

Murphig looked up at me. There was silence for a few moments. "Let me have some of the black juice," Murphig said.

"All right," I said, getting up with deliberate wariness. Murphig only shivered.

I uncapped one of the bottles and set it down within his reach. "I'll get you an eyedropper," I said. As I ducked under the counter to get it I heard him grab the bottle. When I came up he was wiping his mouth.

"Hey!" I said. "Be careful. That stuff is almost pure—it's a lot more powerful than you realize."

"Well, that's good!" Murphig said loudly. "I need its power now." His eyes gleamed in the lantern light and a deadly flush had come to his cheeks.

"Not so loud," I said.

Murphig lowered his voice and began to speak very rapidly. "When I was a little boy in Perseverance I used to look down at the ocean and wonder what was under it, and I would ask my father, and he would say, 'Son, pray to Peace or Truth to allay the pain of your lack of understanding,' and I did, and it didn't help. That was when I committed my first major sin. It was on Remembrance Day, almost ten years ago. I was at the memory banks learning the stories of some of the dead. One of the men I had to remember had vanished at sea. That made me curious and I perverted the use of the memory banks. I looked through them for those who had vanished at sea. Not to remember their spirits, but just for me. And there were hundreds of them. Sinners mostly. Sinners like me."

"Oh?" I said. "Go on."

"That was only the beginning," Murphig said feverishly.

157

"I studied history. I neglected the story of the True Faith for other things, the mysteries. Like the Sundog Year, and the clouds of St. Elmo's Fire. There are dozens of things. The floating islands. The things that crawled up the cliffs during the Hungry Year. Then there was that thing that washed up in the Pentacle Islands, in the old days. They said it was an old dead anemone, all battered and thornless—but there were no stumps. Just four digits like fingers, huge things, and a thumb and a kind of boneless wrist. Fifty feet across. It was a hand, a giant hand." Murphig was breathing hard. He was still clutching his sides.

"I stopped praying. That was a sin, too, my despair. I thought no Fragment would listen to me or my impieties. I tried everything, too—I even prayed to Growth, like the rebels did. That was my worst sin. I'll never forget the shame. But that didn't stop me. Instead I went to sea for myself. With an alien captain. I wanted to find out, you see? I would have been ashamed to go to sea with pious men.

"Then there was the drug. For a while I thought some Fragment of God had sent me that keenness of mind. But instead it was you. You and your friend."

"That's true," I said frankly. "It was a criminal act. It seemed necessary at the time, though."

"It was a *sin*. You should be punished."

"Maybe so," I said. "And no doubt you could cause me a great deal of pain and embarrassment by revealing my actions. However, you just killed a man, so now you're equally vulnerable. That leaves us at a stalemate. I suggest we leave justice to the afterlife. You see how much simpler that is?"

"Your arrogance has made you deaf and blind," Murphig said. "You don't know what the captain is doing—if you could hear his insane plans you would know. I've sinned many times, but never like that. Never like *he* wants me to. I could never do what he asks—not against *Them*.

"We have a common enemy, us Nullaquans and Them. It's you, you aliens. They need us to cover them up, to hide them from the prying eyes of men. And we need them, to *get* people like you, to stop you from changing us, so we

158

can still keep faith with God. I've sinned against stability, and so have you. But I admit it freely. I repent! Do you forgive me?"

I looked at him, feeling an odd stirring of sympathy. "You look terrible, Murphig. Don't worry yourself—it's destructive. Calothrick stumbled overboard, and there's plenty of Flare for both of us. We should be allies; we have more things in common than our sins. Now we'd better get you to your bunk."

Murphig had a coughing fit and there was a wetness to it that alarmed me. "Do you forgive me?" he demanded hoarsely. "Grant me grace! Do you forgive me?"

"You idiot!" I said. "Of course I forgive you."

"Thank God. I feel so sick." He swayed on his stool.

"Look out!" I said, and half caught him as he fell off.

I eased him to the floor. It looked like an overdose—his face had turned as gray as whalehide. He was breathing shallowly. As I checked his pulse I saw a spreading stain on his left side, where his hand had hidden it as he hugged himself. I opened his jacket and shirt, quickly, and I saw the worst . . . the nasty gleam of the broken-off edge of Calothrick's jackknife, jagged and shiny in the blood.

I grabbed the end of the blade with the plierslike gripping edge of a can opener and pulled it out of the wound. I put pressure on the wound with a folded potholder, and stopped the bleeding. I propped up his feet on the lower rung of the stool to help with the shock, and when he stopped breathing I gave him artificial respiration. But he died.

"This is the worst," I told myself. "The absolute worst." I took a small shot of Flare to stop my hands from shaking. I spread my quilt over the body and sat down on the kitchen stool to think my way out of the situation.

There was no help for it. I was going to have to throw Murphig overboard. I couldn't hide him anywhere safely, and there was no sense in leaving him on board with the mark of murder on his side. It was far easier to dump him, so that he could join Calothrick as another mystery of the deep. The double disappearance was not a happy solution to my problem, but it was the safest and simplest.

Once I had made up my mind I saw no point in stalling. I took the quilt off, making sure it hadn't touched the small puddle of blood. Then I heaved the body over one shoulder and climbed ponderously up the stairs. I opened the hatch and looked out. I saw nothing suspicious, so I reeled slowly toward the port rail. I was about to dump him when I thought that the splash might possibly be loud enough to attract attention. It wasn't likely, but I lowered him quietly to the deck and got ready to slide him out head first under the railing.

I heard heavy footsteps. A lantern flared up by the captain's hatch. I froze, but it was too late; he had been watching me.

"What have we here?" the captain said.

Chapter 14

Desperandum Conducts an Experiment

I didn't say anything. Desperandum stooped to peel back Murphig's eyelid with one thick thumb. He brought his lantern close to the dead man's face and studied the eye for a moment. Then he straightened up.

"Syncophine overdose," he said, with a sort of morbid satisfaction. "Written all over his face. Did you murder him, Newhouse?"

I pried my mask slightly away from my face, just enough to make my voice audible. "No," I said, too stunned to dissemble. "He drank too much of it. He was upset because he just killed Calothrick."

"For death's sake," Desperandum said, sounding more annoyed than shocked. "What a stupid, reckless act. Well, Newhouse? Don't just sit there like a lump of suet. Explain yourself."

"Well," I said.

"Don't bother to lie. I know you much better than you think I do. I know all about Flare—do they still call it that? I know about the still in the kitchen, too. And Calothrick's addiction was obvious, at least to an initiate."

I was red-handed and we both knew it, so I said quite frankly, "They got into a fight over Flare. Calothrick stabbed him, but Murphig threw him overboard and the sharks got him. I saw it and offered to help him hide the murder so the Flare thing could stay under cover. But Murphig drank too much Flare and died, and now I have to throw him overboard or be found out. It's not honest, but it's easiest, Captain."

161

Desperandum mulled it over. "It's a dirty shame about Murphig. He could have been very useful to me. Now I'll have to find a replacement for him."

There was a weighty silence. The implication of his statement was obvious.

"What do you want me to do?" I said.

"No conditions," Desperandum said flintily, quite secure in his power. "Are you willing to take his place?"

"Is it honorable?"

Desperandum chuckled in quiet contempt. "By your standards, you mean? Yes. As honorable as anything you've ever done. Now, yes or no?"

"This is absurd! I want to know what—" The captain's expression changed, and just as quickly I said, "I'll do it. Yes."

His cry of alarm was cut off before it was ever uttered, and a bemused expression crossed his face for a few rapid heartbeats. Then Desperandum said, "Very well then, over he goes," and we shoved Murphig under the railing.

The gnashing of the sharks was half-muffled in the roiling dust. Desperandum spoke with loathing. "Death, I hate those monsters. Damn their teeth! But we can't let hate stop progress, can we? I'm going back to bed—as soon as I finish looking over the craft, that is."

"Captain, now that I've agreed—"

"No more, Newhouse. Pull your mask on tight; do you want to ruin your lungs?"

"But I only—"

"Go to sleep. And try to remember you're an innocent man." Desperandum turned off his lantern and thumped off into the darkness.

I went below. My lungs burned, and sleep was slow in coming.

I was up at dawn for breakfast. The two men were missed at mess. There was a perfunctory search of the vessel, and hypocritical displays of deep concern from the captain and myself. Desperandum amazed me; his performance was so authentic that it seemed to hint at a split personality—no uncommon occurrence in a man of his age.

The situation could have been much worse; the two missing men had not been popular. No one cared for Murphig much; his mannerisms were peculiar, and he had come from the wrong social class for a sailor. Calothrick was even less liked; he was a cipher, a sinner, and an off-worlder to boot. In fact, many of the crew seemed to regret that Dalusa had not vanished as well; they had always despised her as a parody of womanhood. No doubt the sailors were profoundly disturbed by the "accident," as it came to be called, but they didn't talk about it much. They didn't talk about anything much.

Desperandum's official theory was that they had fought and fallen overboard, and everyone paid lip service to this idea.

The anxiety caused by the mishap may have accounted for the crew's feverish energy that day. Desperandum soon had them working on the whale. They seemed inspired by the captain's unflagging vitality and they worked like maniacs on this incomprehensible task.

The methodical nature of the process showed the long thought behind it. First the whale was completely hollowed out and its insides cleansed and salted to prevent decay. Its gullet was cleaned out and plugged. Its eyes were dug out with harpoons and replaced with foot-thick lenses of transparent plastic coated with a clear, slippery substance that would retard dust abrasion . . . for a while, at least.

While this was being done Desperandum went into the hold and unlocked his hidden bulkhead. The engine, the tank of oxygen, the tub of glue, and the batteries were all dragged onto the deck.

Desperandum hauled the engine into the body cavity of the whale. Three men bored a long hole inside the whale lengthwise through the tail of the monster. The blacksmiths forged a long propeller shaft for Desperandum, and they thrust it through the hole. While the blacksmiths welded on the propeller Desperandum attached the batteries and started it up. The propeller whirred like a buzz saw.

Satisfied, Desperandum began work on the fins. They

163

were attached to long iron levers inside the animal. The crew members were hardly able to budge them, but Desperandum's double-gravity strength allowed him to wiggle them almost as well as the whale.

Desperandum painted all the outside seals with glue, making them absolutely airtight. He had some problems with the propeller shaft, and the friction would soon wear away even the stout plastic washers and gaskets. But he seemed satisfied.

As we worked together on the day's last meal, Dalusa and I were both remote and uneasy. She had to step aside from the tiny droplets of grease as I fried some meat, and she spoke in her momentary idleness.

"What is he doing, John? What is the captain doing?"

"Dalusa," I said, "I couldn't believe it at first, but its obvious by now that the damned thing's a submarine," and I explained to her the nature of submarines.

"To go beneath the surface? Will he use it?"

"He's been thinking about it a long time," I said, "and I think he's going to ask me to go with him. In fact, I'm almost sure of it."

"You? Both of you?"

"I think so." I said with false cheerfulness.

"But John, why?" she said, alarmed.

I answered offhandedly, "Someone has to take care of the old fellow, don't you agree? He's too careless. Why not me? I understand him, and I'm not afraid."

"But John, it could be dangerous."

"Oh, certainly," I said. "I wouldn't have done it myself. But the captain has his heart set on it, and I have an obligation to go if he asks."

"But you might be killed, John! What then?"

"It's never happened before," I said, but the utter blankness of Dalusa's response showed that my wit had been lost in translation. "It's a little risky," I said, "but I'm a resourseful sort—more so than the captain thinks."

"Oh, John, don't go! The thing that took the crewman last night still might be waiting. Tell the captain to not go!"

"What 'thing that took the crewmen?' Dalusa, don't be absurd. They fell overboard. There's nothing waiting down there." I regretted the words as soon as they were spoken—they struck a chill into me. Dalusa seemed to perk up, though.

"I don't understand mankind," she said. "But this is human, yes? To help someone who needs you, even if it's dangerous—even if it hurts?"

"Yes." I said, nodding sagely. "That's part of it."

"Then, John, good! I can do that. I'm not afraid, either. Some day I will do that, too, and you can be proud of me—like I'm proud of you, John."

"All right, sweetheart," I said. I sniffed. "I think your pastry's burning," I said, and after that I saw to it that we talked of other things.

That night Desperandum called me into his cabin.

"This is it, Newhouse!" he told me excitedly. "I'm going down to see it with my own eyes! I want firsthand contact with the data!"

"That's wonderful, Captain," I said. "A remarkable feat of engineering. It's hollow, though. How will you get it to sink?"

"The crew is storing ballast in it this very minute."

"Then how will you get back to the surface?"

"Easily. Just like flying an airplane. It's also heavier than the medium that supports it, you see? And I have a powerful engine."

"Then how will you get out?"

"I have my axe on board. I'll rendezvous with the *Lunglance* and cut my way out in a matter of seconds."

"And the sharks, Captain?"

"They can't follow me into the depths. I've examined their metabolisms; they're not built for it. This whale is built for better things than they."

"How will you breathe?"

"I have my oxygen mask!" the captain shouted. "I have it all planned!"

"It's an amazing piece of work, Captain," I told him soothingly.

Desperandum looked at me sharply. He got up from his worktable and went to the cabin door. He opened it quickly and looked out, but there was no one there. He shut the door and bolted it.

"I'm glad to see you show so much enthusiasm for the venture," he said. "Because I want you to come with me."

I had expected this and I made a determined effort to talk my way out of it. "Captain, sir," I said, "who financed this expedition? Who worked tirelessly to promote it? Who chose the experiments, carried them out, recorded them? Who made a lasting contribution to human knowledge, gave new insights into the ecology of an entire planet? It was you. My contributions were minimal, not worth mentioning. No, Captain; you honor me too much, you flatter me beyond my worth. What would they say of me? That my reputation was made at the expense of a better man. I'm just a ship's cook, a wanderer far from home, but I have too much pride to sink to such a thing." Aghast at my unconscious pun, I hurried on. "The glory should all be yours, Captain. It belongs not to me, but to Nils Desperandum."

"Ah, but that's where you're wrong," the Captain said slowly. "Desperandum's just a dustmask of a name. The real credit belongs to me—Ericald Svobold."

I was stunned. *"You're* Svobold? The discoverer of—that is—"

"Syncophine, that's right," the captain said mercilessly. "Oh, I gave up using Flare years ago, but I can still recognize a user."

There was silence. I laughed, rather shrilly. "It's ironic, Captain. You know, you've been my idol for years. Why, I've drunk and dropped to your memory a hundred times. But if the legends are right, why, you must be over four hundred years—"

"Let's not get into that," the captain said. "Let's stick to the here and now. When you get to be my age you'll find that's best. Now, I don't know how or why you introduced Murphig to syncophine. I don't know how or why your henchman and my sharpest crewman both died in a single night. Your guilt or innocence is not my concern. But there's no way out for you now, Newhouse. You might as well stop squirming. You know you're caught. I can tell it just

166

by looking at your face. I'm old, all right, but not in my dotage. Oh no. It doesn't happen like that nowadays, not to us galactics. We only get sharper and sharper—God only knows how intolerably sharp we can become. If you could see the things I see for just one day—but that's beside the point.

"I need you, Newhouse. I need a witness. I would have taken Murphig, you see. He was the only man among the crew, the only Nullaquan who could have *understood* the incredible revelations we're going to find down there. The rest of these woodenheads—they don't even have the saving grace of curiosity that Murphig had. So that leaves you, sir."

"But it's not so, Captain," I said. "I'm hardly your most reliable witness. I'm a vagrant. And, yes, I use drugs. You need a solid, down-to-earth sort. First mate Flack for instance."

"Flack has a wife and children," the captain said chillingly. "And he doesn't have half your mental agility. You know, I could almost admire you, Newhouse. I can understand your corrupting Murphig—and liquidating Calothrick, who was a jackal anyway—but I can't understand your leading on Dalusa, that poor tormented creature. That was a vicious act. And I'm offering you a chance to purify yourself, to do something selfless for once. Think of it, Newhouse. Don't you need this as much as I do?"

"You're mistaken," I said. "I *love* Dalusa. When this is over I'm going to take her away—someplace where we can live free from death and madness."

Desperandum looked at me closely for over a minute. Finally he said, "You do love her, don't you? You're in even worse trouble than I thought."

"That remains to be seen," I said. "Captain—Captain Svobold—if the legends are true, you're a man of honor. I still love life, but I'll court death with you if I must. But I want your word that after this there will be no more threats, spoken or unspoken."

"You have my word," Desperandum said. He extended his hand. I shook it, with the whimsical feeling of a nightmare.

167

Then I secured my mask and went up on deck. To starboard, the men were still working on the whale. I went down to the kitchen to sleep.

Next morning, Desperandum was eager to be under way. There was barely time for a brief, tearful farewell to Dalusa before he called me to his cabin. From there, the captain and I walked across the deck toward our odd vehicle with all the dignity we could muster. Through some atavistic social instinct I was still putting a good face on matters, and the captain was the gentleman scientist to the end. Calmly, he shook the hands of his three mates, making them wince. Knowing no better, I shook them too.

"Are you really going down there, Cookie?" Grent asked me as he shook my hand. I nodded. I was already regretting that Grent's voice would be one of my last memories.

"Hope you're back in time for supper," he said. I nodded again, unable to reply because of the mask. I might have denounced the captain otherwise, shouted: "He's crazy, don't you see? He has to be restrained for his own good!" But it wouldn't have worked. The captain would have seen to it that my life was ruined; it would have hurt Dalusa as well.

The captain waved formally to the crew, then ruined the dignity of his exit by clumsily forcing his huge bulk through the slash in the whale's side. "Greasy luck, Captain!" Flack called out as I followed him.

Following their captain's orders, the crew securely glued a great doubled sheet of whaleskin over our entanceway. It grew dark at once inside our musty, eviscerated craft. Soon my eyes adjusted to the dim sunlight pouring through the animal's goggling eye plugs. Desperandum—somehow I could not get used to thinking of him as Svobold—calmly took the ends of the iron fin-levers in his meaty hands.

"I'll navigate for now, Newhouse," he said kindly, giving the fins an experimental wiggle. "You go up for'ard to the portholes and keep the lookout. 'Ware the ballast now."

My eyes had adjusted fully now and everything took on a hallucinatory clarity as I picked my way forward through the heaped-up "ballast." It was an incredible hodgepodge of heavy, miscellaneous jetsam: chunks of pipe, tight-wound bales of wire, bolt buckets, bundles of welding rods, metal boxes heaped with spare parts for the meat grinders, the oven, the recycler, neatly spooled miles of ceramic cable (it amazed me to see yet more of this particular item; Death knows where he kept it all), spare shafts and hafts for harpoons, flensing spades and axes, Desperandum's own mighty axe, and crates containing stacked specimen jars, each one brim-full with murky, yellowish fluid. The whole mess was haphazardly bound together with an a-geometrical webwork of cable, stringing with a loony haphazardness from junk to chunk. As I picked my way forward, noting the neat sailor's knots that bound everything, the floor moved and I pitched forward, striking the plug in the monster's tiny gullet a solid blow with my head.

The crew had not wasted time. I could see their operations through the port plug as they calmly turned the pulleys and cranks that governed the hoists.

As soon as our craft began to lift free there was an ominous series of sinewy creaks, pops and snaps as the inertia tugged the mummified muscle and bone. The thick, leathery belly flesh of the floor bowed noticeably under the weight of the ballast, and the bone-strutted walls leaned inward a little with the groany reluctance of rigor mortis.

There was a muffled hiss as Desperandum turned on the valves to the oxygen mask. Slowly, we swung outwards, off the deck and over the quietly seething sea.

Slowly we went down and settled into the dust with a floury rush and a whisper. There were four muffled thumps as the slings were released, and we began to sink. Desperandum turned on the engine, and it began to whir and mumble. We surged slowly forward. Frothing dust washed quietly over the eye plugs and even as I watched, it grew pitch black inside the sub. I quickly ripped off my mask.

"My death!" I cried out. "It's black! It's completely black! Captain, we can't see a thing!"

"Of course," the captain replied urbanely. "The light can't reach inside, you see. That's why I had our own lights installed." There was a click and wan bluish light from a naked bulb overhead filled the sub. A pale charnel-house

169

radiance gleamed off exposed patches of bone amid the dry sinew of the walls and ceiling.

I sneezed and put my mask back on. The dry mustiness was awful. I returned my attention to the eye plugs. An intricately patterned swirl of dust moved across our lenses, slowly abrading them. I realized with a shock that Desperandum's calmly stated absurdity had momentarily convinced me. I took off the mask again, ignoring the itch of dust in my sinuses. I swallowed to depressurize my ears and said, "Captain. This is ridiculous. The dust is opaque. We might as well be blindfolded."

"Indeed," Desperandum said. He moved the ends of the levers upwards slightly and the sub nose-dived alarmingly. He pulled us back out of it. My ears popped again, and a chorus of creaks spoke up from the musty joints of ribs and vertebrae.

"Take us back up, Captain! The trip's a failure! We can't see anything, so we're risking our lives for nothing. Come now, Captain."

Desperandum looped the oxygen mask over the snouted nozzle of his dustmask and inhaled audibly. The ship rolled and he grabbed his fin levers tightly.

The sounds from his speakers were half-muffled as Desperandum replied. "It's not your job to theorize on the optical properties of dust, Newhouse. Just keep watching. We should reach one of the translucent layers soon."

"The translucent layers! The *translucent* layers? Captain, this is dust, not glass! For death's sake!"

"Really, Newhouse. Your language! I've made a long study of subsurface conditions. You needn't succumb to hysteria. You need some oxygen, that's all."

"I can't understand why I didn't think of this before," I said. "Your insanity must have infected us all." My last words were lost in a long dry groaning of ribs under pressure. The whaleskin glued over the slash in the sub's side was forming a herniated bulge as it dimpled inwards.

"This is absurd," I said, coughing. "I won't be involved in your suicide. I'm going to cut my way out." I picked my way across the tangled ballast toward Desperandum's axe. With an effort I managed to hoist the huge, double-bladed axe to one shoulder. I moved shakily toward the bulging skin, where it would be easiest to cut. The flooring boomed uneasily under my feet.

"I wouldn't do that at this depth if I were you," Desperandum said. "The rush of dust would knock you to a pulp."

I hesitated. "We're not that deep yet."

In answer Desperandum moved the fins and we dived again. I nearly fell down. I set the axe down quickly.

"Now return to your post," he said flatly. I went, pulling my mask back on. The dust in the air and the stench inside the whale were making my nose run. It was impossible to tell our depth. Even the increasing pressure was not a reliable indication, because Desperandum had the oxygen tank open and running. Dust ran thickly by the plugs. My mind raced frantically, trying to squirm out from under a lowering weight of despair. After a while I felt a fatalistic inertia settling into the cores of my bones.

"The air's getting so heavy," I said. "I feel numb all over." I stared out.

"Come get some oxygen then. I've never felt better," Desperandum said.

A small amorphous something slid past the glass. "Wait a minute," I said. "I saw something move just now!"

"What? What was it?" Desperandum said eagerly.

"I don't know," I said. "It was small and wiggly-looking. I think I'd better get some air. I feel drunk."

Desperandum inhaled hugely. "Wonderful, isn't it? Tell you what, my lad. You take over navigation for a while, get some good air in your lungs. Let's see what my trained eyes can make of it."

I stumbled over the ballast, took a fiery gulp of oxygen, and grabbed the levers. I had an absurdly light feeling as I took the levers in my hands, the oxygen mask half-dangling from the snout of my dustmask. Now I could slowly and subtly direct us upward again. Desperandum released the levers, and I immediately knew that the levers were far beyond my strength.

"Captain! Captain!" I said, but my dustmask was on, and the muffled sounds were quickly lost in the drumlike booms of the flooring under Desperandum's boots. It was a silent, desperate struggle then. I put my full weight against the levers and pulled till my wrists ached and cramps bit the insides of my biceps. It was no use. They escaped me, the ends of the levers sweeping violently upward and cracking my dustmask's right lens. We went into an immediate nosedive. Desperandum was crouching at the port eye plug and he fell over immediately. Then the tangled mass of ballast slid onto him like an avalanche. I heard his scream and a yowl of feedback as his speakers shorted out. Then he was lost beneath it all.

I would have fallen on him if I had not been holding the starboard finlever. As it was I dangled about ten feet above him, my feet just above the treacherous, unstable heap of metal and cable and crates. The smell of preserving fluid went through the dry musty air like a knife.

The oxygen tank had taken its mask attachment with it when it tumbled free. The engine, though, was secured to the sub's skeleton, and it had stayed in place. It was still running. Painfully, I pulled myself up the length of the lever until I could wrap my legs around it. Then I pulled off my mask.

"I'm so sorry I came down here," I said. "I'm really, really sorry I did it, and it wasn't my idea at all, and if I ever get away from here I'll never, ever let this happen again—"

"Newhouse . . ."

"—to me or anyone else, ever, ever again. . . ."

"Newhouse. Turn off the engines. Turn them off!"

"Captain! Captain Desperandum!"

"Turn off the engines, Newhouse," came Desperandum's reasonable voice. "I think I hear something down here."

Tears were running down my face. "I don't know if I can do it, Captain," I said. "There's something wrong with me."

"It's nitrogen narcosis, my lad. We're too deep, far too deep. You'll have to turn off the engine. I can't do it. I can't feel my legs."

I shuddered. "All right, Captain. I'll try." I inched my way up the lever, dug my feet and fingers into the stinking,

172

dessicated flesh around the ribs, and leapt. The whirling propeller shaft almost brushed against my face, but I wrapped my arms around the bulk of the engine. I kicked once, twice against the switch, and the engine shut down with a moan and a mumble.

Then there was silence. I heard the crunch and rustle of Desperandum moving amid the rubble. "I can just see out the eyehole," he said. "There. Do you hear that?"

I got up on top of the engine block, and it groaned a little. The whole belly of the hollow whale was bulging inward at my back. "I don't hear anything, Captain. Just the dust . . . I think."

"I see them moving out there," Desperandum said matter-of-factly. "They're quite small. And they're shining—sort of an amorphous glow. There are hundreds of them. I can see them strung off into the distance."

"Captain," I said. "Captain, how are we going to get back to the surface? We can't navigate while the ship is standing on its head like this." I burst into feeble giggles. It was half the nitrogen poisoning, half the pure deadly ludicrousness of the situation.

"That's not important now, Newhouse. But it's vital that you come down here and confirm this sighting. We're making scientific history."

"No." I said. "I'm not going to look at them. They have a right to their privacy. God I wish I had some clean air. I feel so weak."

Desperandum was silent for a while. Then he said coaxingly, "The oxygen's down here with me. I can hear it hissing. You'll pass out in a little while if you don't get some, you know. And maybe you could get these pipes off my legs. I think they're bleeding, but it might just be the preservative fluid. Then you could have a look. Just a little one. What do you have to lose?"

"No!" I said more urgently, my fogged brain stung a little now with panic. "I don't want to look at them. I don't think they want me to."

"For stability's sake!" Desperandum said, resorting to Nullaquan profanity in his final crisis. "Don't you have a shred of plain human curiosity? Just think how *interesting*

173

they are! I never realized they were so *small!* And the way they move is so fascinating, almost a kind of dance. Like little colored lights. See how they move away to the sides now! And—Oh my God!"

Desperandum began to scream. "Look at *that* thing! Look at the *size* of it! It's coming closer! It's coming too close! It's coming too close to us! Don't! Don't do it!"

There was a jar that nearly knocked me loose from the engine. Then a hideous cracking and crumbling. Something was squeezing us. Big dimpled indentations, like troughs, appeared in the back and belly of the whale—five of them. There were four of them across the back and a big thumb-like one almost directly behind me. The great dry bones added their screaming to the captain's. There was a crunch, a scream, a great rupturing sound at the savage bursting of our vessel, a rush and roar of exploding air—grayness—and blackness.

Chapter 15
The Dream

The sky was that blackness, and I was in the sky, floating weightless, disembodied. Far below me, baked in raw sunlight, was the shimmering, seething Nallaqua Crater. And as the landscape cleared, I saw before me a city of the Elder Culture, reborn.

The city was a miracle. It was whole, beautiful, charged with the energy of life, its fluted spires and broad black plazas shrouded from vacuum by a thin protective field, the iridescent essence of a bubble. As I watched I saw delicate, insect-wing tints chase one another across its translucent surface. It was far beyond anything made by man. This was the Elder Culture at its peak.

Something moved me closer. I slipped without difficulty through the field surrounding the city. There was no sense of transition; suddenly I was watching a citizen at work. He was a reptilian centaurlike being, his skin one long sheen of tiny golden red scales. He had eight eyes circling his pink head like studs in a headband.

He sat alone in a small, hexagonal room, lit by a shifting geometric pattern of tiny bulbs in the ceiling. Incense smoldered in a corner. Before him on a low black pedestal was a device that might best be called a sculpture. The core of it was a solid yellow cylinder, shrouded by a blindingly intricate linking and twisting of multicolored beads, glowing like winter stars through a cloud of mist.

I had an intuition that was not my own. I saw the object's significance at once. It was at the same time a work of art, a religious symbol, and a physical representation of its owner's persona.

He looked at the sculpture intently. He was dissatisfied. Out of the thousands of beads, three abruptly winked out. He had just destroyed a month's work.

His latest work had been too rushed, too hurried. The stresses of the past months had affected him subliminally, and true soul sculpture required complete repose.

He wanted peace. Surcease. Electropsychic nirvana, the dynamic joy, the more than religious content that would come when, his personality was fused with the sculpture, and he died. Friends would launch his soul into an infinity of space, to float eternally.

Once this belief had been their faith, but now it was the literal truth. The Elder Culture had made it so.

Changing, I floated from the centaur's room and into the city streets. There was an incredible throng, members of a race that took a pure hedonistic joy in the possibilities of surgical alteration. They switched bodies, sexes, ages, and races as easily as breathing, and their happy disdain for uniformity was dazzling. There were great spiny bipeds; slinking doglike things with the hands of men; big creeping bulks with multiplicities of crablike pincered legs; hairy, globular beings with long, warty, cranelike legs and huge, incongrous wings; things on wheels or tracks with great grapelike clusters of dozens of eyes and ears; things that flew, that slid, that humped, that wallowed; things that traveled in colonies, or linked by long umbilicals, or moved in great multiheaded hybrids like whole families grafted together. It seemed so natural, rainbow people in the rainbow streets; humans seemed drab and antlike in comparison.

But there was fear, an underlying itchy unease, the knowledge that there were enemies below. There had been no opposition to the establishment of the two outposts, which despite their aesthetic qualities were only minor biological waystations. They had been established high above the crater to avoid any possible biocontamination. The first years had gone smoothly, with only the disturbing presence of certain anomalies in the crater to disrupt routine.

Soundings didn't work. The first real trouble came with seismic probing of the depths. Results were inconclusive; then came ominous rumblings from the depths of the crater. It might have been a fault, disturbed by the first explosions, seeking equilibrium. But the shocks seemed to come from random areas at random times.

There was a shift in the patterns of currents in the dust; directly beneath the two outposts, seventy miles down, slow gray vortexes appeared. Probes were sent down to investigate. The dust exhibited a previously unknown quality; apparently acting through static attraction, it leapt out of the air to cling to the probes, smothering them, weighing them down until their engines failed and they fell buzzing into the depths.

The Elder Culture scientists were intrigued. Was there intelligent life in the crater? Radio signals met with no response; after a few months, a heavily armored probe was sent into the dust. It met no resistance; it sank two miles into the black depths, until it hit what appeared to be solid rock. When it tried to move sideways, there was a sudden shock; the sea floor gave way under the probe, and it fell into a blistering pool of magma. Its signals ceased.

A second, temperature-resistant probe was launched. It was being closely followed when a sudden meteorite rain provided a distraction. Power was diverted to the shields; the static from the disintegration of the meteors in the atmosphere below caused a break in contact with the probe. It vanished without a trace.

Now the scientists were nonplussed. While they thought over the situation, there was a sudden, violent explosion across the crater, high above the atmosphere, at the southern edge of the rim.

There was no explanation for it. The smooth, glassy crater-with-the-crater, still partially molten when the outposts investigated, had no traces of radioactivity. There were no meteorite fragments or signs of any chemical explosive. Apparently there had simply been a sudden release of energy from a point source, coming from nowhere, revealing nothing. It was odd that the new crater was of the same radius as the Culture's circular cities. The message was unmistakeable.

The two cities were determined not to overreact. They didn't want to leave the planet, or act with cowardice, or call in a fleet—a distasteful act of aggression. They compromised, deciding to set a large thermonuclear device in stationary orbit over the big crater. In the event of attack it would be a simple, if regrettable process to sterilize the crater. They began work at once.

And the landscape shifted. Beneath the first outpost, something tendril-thin was snaking up the side of the cliff wall. It seemed almost threadlike in the distance, nearly invisible; it was a cylindrical pipe, only six inches wide and the color of a mirror. It was coming from the dust upwards along the wall like the extended tentacle of a monstrous silver octopus. It was apparently in no particular hurry. . . .

Occasionally bulges traveled rapidly up its miles-long length, as if some thick fluid were being pumped upwards in surges inside it. At its very tip, which narrowed to needle sharpness, it moved languidly back and forth along the cliff face, sometimes patting the rock with its sharp blind head, seeming to search, like an earthworm looking for the juiciest part of a corpse. . . . It progressed effortlessly upwards, supporting its miles of exposed length easily, as if gravity were somehow irrelevant. It was already far above the atmosphere, now halfway up the cliff face, now stopping to slide greasily with a snake's speed across a blasted, airless plateau, caressing the rock with its thin, silvered belly.

I was swept closer. Dread seized me. It was forty miles up now, fifty, sixty, still daintily kissing the rock with its pointed, featureless snout. Day came, left, and came again. The snake continued to rise. The rainbow bubble over the city would keep it out, I thought. Nothing could pierce the film as long as the city's generators kept it going. It was only a few miles below the city now. Would the other outpost see it? Or were they too smug to look?

Across the crater I could see the second city. In the cliff face beneath it there was a soundless snap. A hole a yard across appeared in the rock, and an incredible torrent of

178

dust—no, pulverized rock—burst outward like a horizontal geyser. Each particle fell through airlessness like lead, cascading down the cliffside with incredible speed and without cohesion. The geyser slowed to a trickle and dust flowed like water.

And now the silver worm had found something, a thin vertical split in the rock, eight feet high, five inches wide. It slid its narrow head into the rock. Surely the fault was too thin for even its slender body. No matter. The snake slid confidently inward. A bulge came rippling up its sixty-mile length, did not even slow as it entered the crevice. Rock cracked, snapped, and split like hot glass dropped in ice-water. Jagged chips broke out from the cliff, falling soundlessly mile after mile, fathering enough speed to be melted into tektites when they hit the atmosphere below.

Now the snake reversed its rippling, bulges traveling downward mile after mile to vanish in the gray dust sea. Ripple followed ripple like peristalsis, and I realized that whatever lived inside that grotesque metal worm was eating its way upward, invisibly, through the last miles of rock.

Automatic sensors had picked up the dust geyser beneath the second city. An alarm went off; a catlike feathered creature awoke at his console, yawned, stretched, examined the computer's graceful Elder Culture hieroglyphs on a printout screen. He shut off the alarm, blinked sleepy green eyes, and tried to make sense of the information. It looked interesting; he decided to call his superior.

The worm came up in the center of the first city.

The tesselated pavement split, small brown and white tiles snapping and crumbling, and the worm flowed out in the middle of a multicolored crowd. It paid no attention to the screaming, or to the panic flight, even though some citizens tripped over it or stepped on it. Instead, it wriggled quickly across the street, still feeling its way, tapping nastily with its tapered head. It encountered a building, a ten-story white octagon ribbed with blue metal, and suddenly increased its speed, all doubt removed now, moving with the speed of a cracking whip. It circled the building, leapt through an alley, circled another building, smashed

179

through the plastic panes of a geodesic cylinder and killed five of its inhabitants almost incidentally, smashing them against walls and bulkheads to leave them crushed in broad pools of blood: a red puddle, a green puddle, a copper-colored puddle. . . .

It ran and moved and slid with dizzy grace, spearing through some buildings wrapping others in casual helixes of its length, moving through every quarter of the city, crossing its own path a hundred times in a drunkard's walk of fear, until at last it returned to its point of origin at the city center. There at the crumbled hole a huge being, a metal-hoofed satyr at least eight feet tall, was stamping repeatedly on the body of the worm. He must have weighed over a ton and the hooves on his bristled legs were sharp, but it was like stamping on a bar of stainless steel.

It was all happening at once. Smoke rose in the eastern part of the city, where a group of citizens had tried to use a radiation weapon on a segment of the worm. The beam had glanced off, melting a dozen bystanders and most of a building. Elsewhere, despairing citizens threw themselves into incompleted soul sculptures, convulsing as sections of their psyches were shorn away. Others made frantic attempts to supply a ship for takeoff. Yet others were beginning to radio warnings and pleas for help to their sister city.

The snake stopped. It was convoluted, wrapped around and through the city's buildings like a tapeworm through intestines. Now it took up the slack. A barely perceptible trembling shook it. Metal began to buckle. Masonry disintegrated. The length of the snake went through buildings like a wire garrote through a human throat, spilling water, hemorrhaging electric fire as it cut through cables and conduits, messily severing dozens of trapped inhabitants, toppling buildings onto the crowds in the streets.

Then it began to retreat down through its hole, sliding slickly inwards like the extended tape from a tape measure. The satyr was still stamping insanely. With its last few yards, as a final gesture, the worm looped itself around and around him, ignoring his wrenching, twisting hands. Then it squeezed him till he burst.

Hundreds had died, but dozens survived, hidden underground or in buildings strangely untouched. There was one cargo ship in the city still functioning; its cyborg pilot had had the great presence of mind to leap the coil as it slithered around the ship. The ship's reactionless drive had curdled a building nearby with great loss of life. But the ship, with its cargo of refugees and hastily salvaged soul sculptures, was intact.

The ship was already trying to pick up survivors when the snake slithered out of the crevice in the side of the cliff and collapsed downward, simply falling, threadlike, in mile-long loop after loop after loop. . . .

The city's atmosphere immediately began to rush out the hole. A cloud of frost appeared as moist air puffed out and froze, glittering in raw vacuum sunlight like the dust of diamonds.

The rainbow film that roofed the city began to collapse as the air whistled out from under it. It settled slowly, dents and ripples forming on its surface, pale bands of insect-wing color chasing one another faster and faster across its surface. Soon it would touch the top of the highest remaining skyscraper.

The second city was in a state of frantic activity now, readying rescue craft, searching for weapons. The first rescue ship was about to lift off when a subtle grinding registered on the outpost's seismographs, a grinding from directly beneath the city.

A circular area all around the outpost suddenly gave way, as neatly as coring an apple. The city immediately fell fifty feet. Rock met rock with incredible impact. There were strong buildings in that city; some of them actually remained standing. But the rainbow film instantly gave way, and a sparkling gust of air leapt upward and outward from the newly formed crater. It was a mercy, really; the freezing vacuum ended the pain of these few still alive. A little disturbed dust, loosened by wind, sifted over the freezing ruins like a scattered benediction.

There were no witnesses. The rainbow film on the first city was still collapsing. A final long indentation touched the leaning top of a battered skyscraper. Blinding white energy sleeted outward from the area of contact; the top of the building dripped hot slag into the street. The film burst.

Death was immediate. Even as the few survivors died in their underground shelters, coughing blood of different colors, the last starship lifted off. Its reactionless drive, at frantic full power, melted a few of the remaining buildings, and it surged away from the planet's surface. Seeking free space.

A cloud of dust arose from the crater beneath, a small cloud, no more than two or three tons worth.

It accelerated upwards. I estimated that by the time it reached the lip of the cliff it was doing at least three-quarters of the speed of light. It moved faster than perception; there was no evidence of its existence at all until the hull of the starship was suddenly turned into something like metal cheesecloth. The loss of air was only incidental. Everyone aboard was riddled with charred holes, thousands of them. There was no blood; it was all cauterized. And they were all dead.

The hulk drifted off serenely into blackness.

The sun was setting over the rim of the Nullaqua Crater. The sea below was calm; the slow vortexes of dust that had disturbed its surface stilled into eddies and vanished. The whole Crater seemed to settle into the peace of complete satisfaction, a state like the quiet joy of drawing in one's first cool breath when a fever has finally broken. Stasis. Peace. Stability.

The sound of coughing woke me.

I opened my eyes to a vast unfocused glare, and blinked away a gritty film of tears. The dust was all over my face, clogging my eyelids, crusting inside my nose, coating the inside of my mouth with a nauseating mealy dryness. I was floating on my back on the surface of the sea.

I tried to clear my mouth. My lips split their dusty scabs and thickened blood flowed over my dessicated tongue. My mouth revived a little in the wetness and saliva began to flow, turning the dust to a thick nastiness. I began coughing convulsively.

My dustmask was still hanging by a strap around my neck. When I reached for it I felt the first red-hot jolt of pain penetrate the numbness of shock. I felt it like a burning bubble inside my right elbow. As I moved weakly others sprang up like flames in my joints and muscles—knees, thighs, arms. Tears of agony channeled through the dust on my cheeks. I had the bends.

An aeroembolism in my heart could kill me. I lay very still, feeding the dust with the tears clearing my eyes and the blood oozing through caked clots from wounds in legs and hands and ears. I tried to control my coughing; I was beginning to suffocate. I reached for my mask again and felt red-hot spikes rip through bones and nerves and tendons. I realized that death was very near, and the thought called up deep reserves of animal vitality.

I spat wet sludge and said, "I want to live. Just let me live. I can help you, I'll be your friend . . . you gods . . ."

I reached for my mask left-handed, and the pain was not so bad. As I lifted the mask to pour the dust out of it, my head sank a little and I was forced to kick my legs to keep my face from going under. My knees and hips began to burn from the inside out, little trapped fires boiling under my kneecaps. My hands trembled uncontrollably as I put the dustmask to my face. Its adhesive edge, form-fitted to my face, pushed grit into my skin. I wheezed outward to clear the filters. Dust fell from the little rubbery creases around the lenses, inside the mask, to torment my nose and eyes. I lay still again, waiting for the pain to burn itself out.

In the absolute stillness there was a sort of numb stasis of pain. But when I moved, it seemed as though my movement cracked a shell around the pain and let it ooze out, burning cells and nerves.

I kept weeping, and my eyes began to clear again. I turned my head a little to look at the cliffs, expecting to find them red with evening—it seemed as if hours had passed—but they were gleaming white.

As I looked I saw a black speck move slantwise across their mighty faces.

The black speck was a disturbing presence in a world of

walls and bitter dust. It was Dalusa. I lifted my left arm, crusted gray on gray. Could she see the movement amid the miles of bleakness? I could barely move my right arm. Beyond the burning nexus in my elbow was the hot mashed numbness of bleeding fingers. I kicked my legs, raising a little plume of dust, clenching my teeth with a crunch of grit at the stabbing pain in my knees.

There was hope. I kicked and splashed in the dust for as long as I could, stopping when I had to fight a choking fit. My eyes kept oozing tears; I felt more than saw the shadow flit across me. There was wind, and the dust slurred over my cracked lenses and Dalusa settled into the dust beside me.

She knelt in the dust, sinking into it waist-deep and stabilizing her position with the extended edges of her wings, like outriggers. She stretched out her pale hands over my face, put the heels on her hands together, crooked her fingers like fangs and meshed them together, once, twice.

There was no mistaking that gesture—sharks. She pointed their direction, half-sinking as she did so.

"It's all over then," I said inside the mask, but she must have heard only a mumble. She swam around to my head with quick sculling motions of her wings. She took my left hand and gently wrapped it around her left ankle. Then she tried to fly.

Her impetus broke my grip at once. As I turned over onto my stomach, wallowing in the dust, I saw a flash of green zip by. Dalusa flinched aside, then snapped out with one preternaturally long arm, snatching a pilot fish out of the air. I heard the rattle of its thin wings against her wrist as she quickly, reflexively, bit through its spine. She threw it aside, and pointed behind me.

I got my hands together and grabbed her ankle in a double panic grip.

She couldn't quite fly; my weight was too much for her. Instead she flopped and splashed and swam, dust bursting up in dirty plumes beneath her. She would leap upward from the dust to fly foward with great powerful surging strokes, fall to dust again, scrabble and swim with wings and hands and her free leg, and leap up once more to fly

184

through the hot, sterile air as if she had to rip her way through it.

We didn't look back. The pain in my arms was filling up the whole crater and spilling out over its edges. I felt fresh blood on my palms, and the slickness of sweat. I felt the skin of Dalusa's ankle beginning to blister, its texture roughening as her skin was devoured with hives.

I couldn't see the blistering because of the dust. I like to think that I would have let her go if I had seen it, accepted my own death rather than hurt her.

But we were always at our best when pain united us. I wanted to live—for her sake almost as much as my own, for the hope we could give each other. In my pain and confusion I could hardly comprehend the sacrifice she was making. It was only later that I grew to understand it.

I didn't let go until we stopped moving. I didn't know how long she had been towing me. It felt like days or weeks. I felt the harshness of rope around my chest, I felt it tighten around my ribs, and, as the sailors hauled me up out of the dust to the deck of the *Lunglance,* I blacked out.

I was vaguely aware of movement beside me before I awoke.

"Here Mr. Cookie. Drink some of this." Meggle, the cabin boy, was holding a ladleful of thin, yellowish broth. I lifted my head and tried to steady the end of the ladle. When I saw the bluish, broken nails of my right hand I started and spilled a little of the broth on my quilt. I drank the rest, feeling the flat saltiness of it sting my mouth and soothe my raw throat. Meggle set down a kettle of it.

"Drink it all," he said. "Mr. Flack says you need lots of water."

I sat up, wincing at the pain in my hand. Someone had sponged the dust off me. I was naked under the quilt. "What time is it?" I said, almost croaking.

"Clifflight."

I drank some more soup. "So I'm rescued," I said. I started to cough rackingly and dropped the ladle with a clatter on the kitchen floor. Innocently, Meggle picked it up and handed it back to me.

"Have you seen anything unusual?" I asked him at last.

185

"Anything big moving under the dust—sharks—like that?"

Meggle looked at me incuriously. "No," he said. He seemed unhappy with my questions, as if my forcing him to answer was an imposition.

"Well, what about Dalusa? Is her leg all right?"

"I dunno Mr. Cookie," Meggle said, reaching up uneasily to tug at a strand of his coarse and incredibly dirty-looking hair. "I only saw its leg when it brought you in. Then it flew off to look for the captain."

"No!" I said, stricken.

Meggle ducked his head guiltily into hunched shoulders. "Mr. Flack tried to stop it," he said. "But it said it had to go look while it still had the strength. Its leg was really awful-looking, all swelled up past the knee and everything, but it said it had to go look for him. The captain I mean. It said it had to find him before the sharks bit all his blood out. That's just what it said: 'Bit all his blood out.' Mr. Flack *tried* to stop it." Meggle looked away.

"How long has she been gone?"

"Three . . . hours."

"Then we might as well go home," I said. "We might as well all go home. She won't be back."

"It might, Mr. Cookie. Mr. Flack put bandages on it and stopped the bleeding. Are you all right, Mr. Cookie? Your eyes are red as fire."

I couldn't say anything. I only waved him away as I looked down into the soup kettle. Meggle put on his mask and went up the stairs out on deck. Salt tears fell into my broth, adding a lingering bitterness to my lonely meal.

It was her last act of faithfulness to those who hurt her, a last misguided act of sham humanity. She must have found the captain, because she never came back.

Chapter 16
The Voyage Ends

My recovery was rapid. I stopped coughing after the first day, and my hearing wasn't affected, even though my ears had bled. I would bear scars on my palms and shins, but only until I could get to a cosmetic surgeon off planet. The other scars were not so quick to heal; they would stay until the passage of time wore my personality away.

When I rifled Desperandum's cabin I discovered that he had had more money than any of us had suspected. Luckily some superstition kept First mate Flack from sleeping in the dead man's quarters. Perhaps he still felt guilty about Desperandum's notebooks.

We had thrown all of Desperandum's notebooks overboard. Flack protested, but only mildly, when I explained to him that their destruction had been the captain's last wish. While lying in my sickbed I had invented a detailed and elaborately worked out lie about our submarine voyage: how our navigation had failed us, how we became mired in the layer of sludge below the surface; the captain's bitter regret and his request that I destroy the evidence of his folly, should I escape; our destruction of the ship; my rescue. My artistry was entirely wasted on the crew; they accepted the explanation without enthusiasm, without even caring.

It was very sad, as sad as watching the abandoned notebooks sink slowly astern, their close-crowded pages riffling slowly in the sluggish breeze. I had watched them long after the crew had returned to their scrimshaw and their silent pursuits.

Even with bruised and swollen hands it was not difficult to break into the cabinet and take the money. To be quite frank, I might have done it in any event; but with Dalusa's death, the money became a kind of wergild. I was able to skim enough off the top to take me away from the planet, while leaving enough for the crew's wages and even a bonus.

We reached the Highisle in two days. Desperandum had left no will, and Flack, as captain, left as soon as we docked to report the situation to the maritime Synod. They would probably give him the ship. It was highly unlikely that Desperandum had heirs on Nullaqua, and the government would frankly not bother with locating any interstellar ones.

I was soon paid off, with a generous bonus. I had thought that Flack would quietly squirrel away a large part of what was left of Desperandum's money; he needed capital, after all. But whether it was some superstitious dread, respect for Desperandum's departed spirit, or plain dumb honesty, he paid us all off handsomely.

I took the elevator up to the city. My first act was to buy a new suit of clothes. I discarded my tattered, repellent whaler's outfit in a recycling chute at the tailor's. Then I reclaimed the goods I had put into storage. With rings on my fingers and my dustmask sold back to a shop for scrap, I felt almost my old self again. But not exactly: there was an unreal quality to it, as if I were haunted by the frail and friendly ghost of my old self.

I walked along Devotion Street, an airy boulevard devoted mostly to restaurants. I let the bright Nullaquan sun touch my face, pale from months behind a mask. I stopped at an outdoor table at one of the restaurants. I had traded in my duffel bag for a smart suitcase. I opened it and took out my only keepsake from Dalusa: a single strand of her hair that I had found in her tent. I didn't dare handle it often, for fear that it would disintegrate, so I usually kept it coiled up inside a little metal canister. Later I had it encased in plastic as a memento.

I put the strand back into the suitcase and closed it. I ordered a beer. As I drank it I felt an attack of loneliness.

Normally I was self-sufficient, and the sudden sharp stab surprised me. Perhaps it was the lingering pain of Dalusa's death; the image of her perfect face swam before me. When she had gone for the last time, she took a great deal of me with her; I felt scoured inside, hollow and in need.

The rational thing to do would have been to go straight to the starship terminal and buy a ticket on the first ship out.

But I felt a sudden urge to visit the New House. The long months, the manifold catastrophes had partially erased my grievances. When the facts were faced, the New House was all I had for a home, its inhabitants were the nearest things I had to friends. I owed it to myself to see them; I owed it to them to warn them about meddling in Nullaqua's frightening cultural symbiosis.

There was also the prospect of vengeance, surprisingly sweet. It might be dangerous to taunt them with my supply of syncophine, perhaps the last left in the Highisle. But they all had money. An extravagant payment would go far toward modifying my resentment. And I was lonely.

Accordingly, I took a commuter train to Piety Street and walked four blocks to the New House. It was dusk, but none of the lights were on. My mind was suddenly thronged with suspicions. My own withdrawal symptoms had been sharper than I liked to admit, and it suddenly struck me the reserves of Flare at the New House must have gotten awfully thin. Perhaps they had lacked the restraint to ration their last gallon properly.

I began to have severe misgivings. I repressed my fantasies and tried the door; it was unlocked.

It was dark inside. I turned on the light. The living room was a shambles. The couch had been gutted, its meager stuffing showing at a dozen places. Dust was thick on the carpet. The chairs were gone.

My nostrils, sensitive from long deprivation, detected a faint, sick-sweet rotting odor. I followed it into the hall, stepping over the shattered remains of Simon the poet's lute.

The odor was strongest by the hall closet. I jerked it open. The released stench was overwhelming; my gorge rose. Huddled in the bottom of the closet, his throat slashed, was old Timon Hadji-Ali. He had finally met the death he sought so avidly. His eyeballs, wide and staring, were covered with a thick patina of dust. His lined, senescent face was slightly bloated from decomposition; a blackened tongue showed between teeth exposed in a death grin. He had been dead for several weeks.

I began to search the rest of the house. A telltale stench warned me at the door to Mr. and Mrs. Undine's room.

At last I gave in to morbid curiosity and opened it. They had hung themselves. No one had bothered to cut them down, but they had long since ceased to sway. They were nude, and still linked in a necro-erotic embrace. Their arms were loosely tied around one another at the wrists. Someone had helped them do that. Soneone had also dug the implanted jewels out of their bodies with a knife. Their barrel chests were spotted with shallow, blackened wounds.

I shut the door, breathing slowly.

All the toilets in the house were clogged and stinking. I went into my own room. Everything I owned had been stolen, except for my best suit of clothes. Those clothes were spread-eagled in the center of my double bed, pinned to the musty mattress with a knife through the heart of my empty jacket.

I went straight for the syncophine, uncapped one of the bottles, and took a small sip. Chemical frenzy dug into my brain; with chattering teeth, I took the bottles out of my suitcase.

Carrying all four bottles, I went back to the hall closet. "Here, Timon," I said, handing him one of the bottles. "Sorry it took me so long."

I went to the Undines. It was easy to stick two of the bottles into their stiffened hands. "I won't be needing these," I said. "I'd like you two to have them."

I went to my bedroom. I took one of the empty sleeves and folded it gently over the last bottle. "Here, John," I said. "You deserve this, since you fought for it so hard, and so long, too. I'm sorry it was so hard to get—I'm sorry for all you dead people."

190

I got my suitcase, left the house, and locked the door behind me.

I had always filled the emptiness with drugs. Now I had withdrawal symptoms to look forward to, and a harrowing reeducation in the meaning of pain.

I'd live. I'd endured worse in the days that drove me to discover drugs in the first place. I had no illusions about drugs; they held no romantic haze. They were just a way to make the mind work differently. The mind, the me, was still there, mutable, magical, no matter what friendly poisons subjected me to their kindly attack. I was strong; my friends had been weak. We had all been crippled, but they had allowed themselves to be devoured by their own carnivorous crutches.

I drew no grim moral lessons, made no rash vows. It was only a misfortune, an accidental trap set by witless Confederates. If my friends deserved punishment, it was only for lack of moderation.

Moderation was survival. Sometimes moderation could only be achieved by an act of fanaticism. I was leaving before Flare began exacting payment for the joy it had given me, removing myself bodily before it could put me further in its debt. I would suffer on a starship.

I had to leave. Relying on willpower was the height of stupidity; it could not stop me from falling back into my old personality patterns. Cold turkey withdrawal would send me burrowing after the guts of dustwhales as irresitably, as blamelessly as iron leaps for a magnet.

Surely it was only a matter of time until I found something else to fill the aching vacuum: truth or duty, honor, beauty, love or wisdom, something. . . .

I thought about it at the starport, sitting on a whalehide chair and watching two emaciated Confederate officers playing chess. Somewhere a purpose awaited me, in the long centuries before Death claimed me, if he could.

For a start, I would visit Venice.